Billionaire Unwed

A BILLIONAIRE'S OBESSION NOVELLA

Zeke

J. S. SCOTT

Contents

Prologue

Lia

Seven Years Ago...

"I love you."

The words had just...fallen out of my mouth. I hadn't stopped to think about them, nor was I worried about how my best friend, Zeke Conner, would interpret the statement.

In my more-than-slightly-inebriated state, I just didn't care about what might happen tomorrow. Or the next day. I was in some kind of lovely live-in-the-moment reality, and the only thing that seemed to matter was finally letting Zeke Conner know *exactly* how I felt.

I had no idea *why* it was suddenly of the utmost importance that Zeke be informed that he was not only my best friend, but the subject of every single erotic fantasy and wet dream I'd ever experienced over the last several years.

I'd done a very good job at keeping those carnal secrets to myself *before* I'd gone barhopping with Zeke tonight, and sampled what seemed like every single cocktail in a bartender's handbook.

Was it so important because I would have *never* said those words had I not been three sheets to the wind, and I wanted to get them out before I was sober again?

Yeah, most likely.

Sober, I was almost certain that my fear of losing Zeke as a friend would keep me silent. I'd just keep pretending like I didn't want to get down and dirty with the guy who had been my best friend and confidant since I was barely fourteen years old.

But I'm not that adoring kid anymore, that girl who had initially looked up to Zeke like he's some kind of protective big brother.

It was my twenty-first birthday, dammit. Even though Zeke would probably always be my hero, it had become absolutely impossible *not* to see him as the hottest guy on the planet, too.

"I love you, too, my adorable, drunken little friend," Zeke answered indulgently as he hoisted me onto my bed.

I watched as he patiently removed the stupid high-heeled shoes that had hindered my ability to walk on my own in the first place.

Maybe wearing those fuck-me shoes had been a big mistake. I was more of a comfortable sneakers kind of female, so my practice at prancing around in a pair of high stilettos was somewhat limited. I think I'd done okay at the beginning of the evening, but somewhere around my third drink...or was it my fourth?...I'd started to get a little wobbly.

"Better?" Zeke asked as the second shoe hit the floor, and he started rubbing the arches of both of my feet.

A tiny whimper of pleasure escaped from my lips as his strong fingers dug into those aching muscles for several minutes before he finally tucked my body between the covers, and pulled the sheet and comforter over me.

"Zeke? Did you hear me say that I love you?"

"Yep," he acknowledged as he sat down on the bed. "I told you that I loved you, too, Jellybean. Did you miss that?"

I grimaced as he grinned down at me, making it perfectly obvious that he was just humoring me.

Okay, maybe I needed to try again, so he'd *really* understand what I meant. "I want to *have sex* with you," I confessed, my words sounding a little slurred, but he *ought* to get what I meant *this time,* right? How much blunter could I possibly get?

His grin grew ever broader. "Everybody wants to have sex when they're drunk, Lia, and honestly, sometimes we're not all that picky about how or who that happens with when we're shitfaced."

I frowned at him. Here I was, spilling my guts to him, and he *wasn't* taking me seriously. At all. Judging by the teasing smile on his face, he wasn't buying a word I said.

I sighed, and shot him a displeased glare.

Okay, so maybe he had good reason for doubting the words of a drunk woman.

I folded my arms across my chest, meeting Zeke's sexy blue-eyed gaze with my own stubborn stare of determination. "I don't want to have sex with you just because I'm drunk," I informed him. "You might be my best friend, but I'd have to be blind not to notice how ridiculously gorgeous you are, too. I don't want to just have sex with *anybody* because I'm plastered. I only want to have sex with *you.*"

A small smile still lingered on those sexy lips of his as he leaned down and kissed my forehead. "I'm damn glad it's me who's with you right now, Jellybean," he mumbled against my skin. "Any other guy would have you naked and on your back right now."

I grasped the front of his button-down shirt with one hand before he could move away, and used the other to poke an exasperated index finger into his chest. "Will you please stop calling me that ridiculous nickname, and stop treating me like a child who has no idea what I want," I huffed indignantly.

Zeke had been calling me *Jellybean* since I was fourteen, and he'd discovered my love of almost every flavor of Jelly Bellies. Okay, so maybe I *still* had a thing for those stupid gourmet jelly beans, and a flavor I associated with almost every emotion or occasion, but I was over that silly nickname.

I watched as his expression changed, his face so close to mine that I could feel his warm breath as he let out a masculine sigh. "I never realized the nickname hurt you, Lia," he said huskily. "It was never meant as anything more than a term of endearment."

My heart somersaulted inside my chest as his tender, contemplative gaze swept over me. I had a love/hate relationship with *that look*.

I loved the fact that Zeke always cared enough to try to read my emotions.

And…I hated it because I'd never seen anything except concerned friendship in that assessing glance.

Exasperated, and remorseful that I'd snapped at him, I released his shirt and let him move away. "You never hurt me, Zeke, and sometimes I like it when you call me Jellybean because I know it's meant to be…affectionate," I confessed. "I guess I'm just being pissy because I'm trying to tell you something from my heart, and you're treating me like I have no idea what I'm talking about."

I shivered as he reached out and pushed a wayward lock of blonde hair from my eyes, his fingers gently brushing my cheek as he performed the loving gesture. "You're out of your head, Lia. You know I have complete respect for anything you have to say, but I was also the guy who watched you put away nearly as many drinks as a college frat boy could handle tonight. So yeah, maybe I'm not taking you seriously at the moment because I've been just as shitfaced as you are right now, and when I was, nothing I said really made sense. I'll be surprised if you even remember any of this tomorrow."

I rolled my eyes like a sulky adolescent, and flopped back onto my pillow. I shot Zeke a look that probably would have killed him if the daggers coming from my eyes were actually real weapons.

Unfortunately, Zeke didn't even flinch at my furious stare. "Have I mentioned how adorable you are when you're drunk angry?" he asked, his deep baritone so cajoling that I knew he was trying to tease me out of being pissed off.

I didn't answer.

"Come on, Lia," he coaxed. "You know it kills me when you're angry at me. Give a guy a break. I did carry you when your feet got tangled up with your high heels, right? Not that I'd ever mind carrying you when you couldn't walk, but you could at least toss a couple of brownie points in my direction."

I pulled my gaze away from his face because I *knew* what was coming. The two of us rarely had big disagreements, but on the rare occasions when we had, Zeke would hound me relentlessly until he found a way to get me laughing again.

It had never taken him very long to accomplish that mission, either. One glance at the silly, puppy dog look he always used to get me to relent usually did the trick.

Damn those sexy eyes of his that could speak volumes without him saying a single word. Once those slightly pleading baby blues caught and locked onto my gaze, I always caved in like a building that had been hit with a massive amount of dynamite.

Not. This. Time.

My eyes stayed stubbornly planted on my bedroom wall. I didn't feel like laughing right now.

He got to his feet. "Okay, so maybe you need a little more time?" he asked hesitantly before he started to stroll toward the bedroom door.

"Where are you going?" I yelled irritably to his retreating figure before I flopped back against my pillow.

"I'll be back," he called.

I tried to decide if the bed was really starting to spin, or if it was just my imagination, as I listened to him rummage around in the kitchen.

It wasn't like it was difficult to hear every move he made.

My new apartment was tiny, but I loved it. I'd just moved out of my grandmother's house a few weeks ago because I'd gotten promoted to manager at the coffee shop I worked in.

Someday, I desperately wanted to open my own place, but in the meantime, I was learning everything I could about the business of all things coffee. When the time came for me to launch my own store, I was going to be ready, and I planned on giving customers a coffee paradise that would keep bringing them back for more.

I sighed as Zeke sauntered back into the room. It wasn't easy having a male best friend who looked like *him*. Especially not when I wanted to be so much more than just his friend. *How could I not?* He was so damn hot that just looking at him was torture. His thick, sandy hair was just willful enough to be sexy rather than messy, and it was still hard to decide if Zeke's hair was light brown or blond. Truthfully, it was both, and those various shades and highlights threaded together so naturally that he could be classified as either one. Add a pair of soulful blue eyes that seemed like they were ever changing from indigo to turquoise. Top those off with a strong jawline, great bone structure, and *that* was Zeke Conner.

Really, with a face like his, was it fair that he'd been blessed with a body worth salivating over, too? He was tall, broad, and incredibly fit. He wasn't bodybuilder muscular. I knew he wasn't into pumping iron, but Zeke was ripped because there were very few physical activities that he didn't enjoy and excel at while he was doing them.

Honestly, putting the fact that the guy had won the genetic lottery aside, one of Zeke's most endearing qualities was the fact that he was just an all-around…nice guy. Unlike some other gorgeous guys I'd met, Zeke wasn't focused on his physical appearance, nor did he act like he noticed that he turned a lot of female heads whenever we went anywhere together. He was that guy who'd do anything he could to help a friend or a perfect stranger. The kind of man anyone would be lucky to call their friend.

Someone I've always been fortunate to call my best friend.

There were so few things that I couldn't discuss with Zeke. He'd push me up when I was down, laugh with me when I was happy, and support me when I needed someone to be there for me. Maybe the only thing I'd never been straight with about was the way my feelings had changed for him over the years.

Correction, I'd never been able to share that with him…until tonight. Which, apparently, might as well have never happened since Zeke didn't believe me, anyway.

"I know you're probably still mad at me, but drink some of this, and take these," he insisted as he sat on the bed and handed me a bottle of water. He put a few more bottles on the bedside table.

I held my hand out unsteadily, and he took it so he could tuck the aspirin into my palm and close my fingers around them.

I took the pills because he seemed to be waiting for me to do it, and gulped down some healthy slugs from the water bottle he handed me.

He nodded toward the bottle with an expectant look. "Drink water as long as you're awake. Lots of it. It will help flush the alcohol and toxins out of your system. I'll be back in the morning with some food, whether you want to talk to me or not," he said gruffly. "You'll probably end up with one hell of a hangover, so you'll need to put something into your stomach in the morning."

I blinked as I looked at him, trying to stop the tears that were suddenly welling up in my eyes from falling. He was obviously done with trying to tease me out of silence, and it didn't take a completely functioning brain for me to sense that he was actually...hurt.

Zeke and I had always had some kind of weird connection that felt like we could actually pick up on each other's emotions. Not in some odd psychic way. The bond was more instinctive than other-worldly, a unique closeness between two people who really cared about each other.

My heart sank, and I hated myself for being a bitch to the one person who'd been there for me every single time I'd needed him. The friend who was *still* trying to take care of me even though I'd hurt his feelings.

Maybe we weren't lovers.

Maybe Zeke would never want me the same way I wanted him.

Maybe it was painful to look at him sometimes and know that we'd never be anything more than best friends.

But...I'd rather suffer through some of that crap than not have Zeke in my life *at all*.

"I'd better take off," Zeke said awkwardly as he rubbed his hands over his jean-clad thighs before he started to stand.

"Don't," I said in a breathless voice as I put a hand on his forearm. "I'm not angry anymore, Zeke. I was just frustrated because I was talking, but I felt like you weren't hearing me."

"Oh, I heard you," he said with patient humor in his tone. "But I know it's the alcohol talking, Lia."

"It's not." Impulsively, I wrapped my arms around his neck. "I want you, Zeke. I have for a long time. I've just been afraid to say it."

I felt his shoulders tense. We were suddenly face-to-face, so close that all I had to do was close the minimal distance between us and I'd finally have his mouth on mine.

Wanting Zeke had become a habit I couldn't break, and a dream I couldn't seem to stop coveting.

His blue eyes turned stormy and turbulent as he stared at me. "It's not happening, Lia. I wanted to take you out to the bars so that I could watch out for you on your birthday. I don't want this, and neither do you. Being drunk makes everything look different. You won't feel the same way in the morning. Trust me. I'd rather have you angry right now than for you to hate me for the rest of your life because I took advantage of you when I knew you were hammered."

I closed my eyes as he leaned forward and kissed my forehead in the same friendly way he always did.

Disappointment flooded my entire being. He was wrong. I *wasn't* going to feel differently in the morning. I'd learn to hide my emotions again when it came to Zeke, but those feelings would *always* be there. I could only hope that when I was sober, I'd be capable of burying them so deeply that they never saw the light of day again.

He gently tugged my arms away from him and stood as he grumbled, "Your phone is on the bedside table. Call me if you need me."

I already needed him, but he'd just firmly and soundly pushed me away. "Okay," I mumbled, feeling totally dejected.

Leave it alone, Lia. It's not his fault that he doesn't feel the same way. If all he wants is friendship, just be his friend. It's better than losing him completely.

Zeke didn't say another word as he exited the bedroom. I heard the apartment door open and close a few moments later.

I had no doubt he'd locked up since he had a key, and Zeke was nothing if not thorough in his desire to make sure I was always safe.

I flopped back onto my pillow again, and instantly regretted the abrupt motion because it made me dizzier than hell.

My emotions were running rampant, and now that Zeke was gone, I didn't even attempt to suppress any of them. Tears leaked from my eyes as I realized how much it hurt that I'd just been soundly rejected by the guy I wanted more than anyone else in the world.

He doesn't want me back.

I let out a strangled sob, and then another, releasing all my pain and tormented grief before I literally cried myself to sleep.

The next morning, Zeke *did* come back with breakfast, just like he'd promised, and I was definitely hung over.

My feelings for Zeke hadn't changed, but I *was* mortified that I'd confessed them all to *him*, and even more embarrassed because he'd very firmly let me know that he didn't see me as anything other than a friend.

For God's sake, I'd blatantly thrown myself at him, and forced the poor guy to back away in utter horror.

I knew Zeke *thought* I didn't remember what had happened the night before, and because it eased my embarrassment, I wasn't about to correct that false assumption.

Zeke and I were friends. Good friends. Best buddies. And the line I'd crossed the night before was horrifying to me the following morning, once the liquor wasn't taking away all of my inhibitions anymore.

I stuffed the adolescent emotions I'd revealed the night before back inside me so forcefully that I knew I'd *never* bring up the subject again. Like it or not, I *had* to accept that Zeke and I weren't meant to be anything other than best friends. Ever.

I had Zeke's friendship, and because he wanted nothing to do with a more intimate relationship, our *friendship* was always going to have to be enough.

I couldn't say that I didn't feel a little awkward after my drunken confession, but a week later, Zeke's college break was over, and he headed back to Harvard.

I threw myself into work, hyper focused on my own goals.

Luckily, the mistake I'd made on my twenty-first birthday was soon just a crappy memory that I didn't allow myself to think about, and my friendship with Zeke remained solid.

Staying in the friendship zone *was* enough for many years. I managed to successfully convince myself that my carnal feelings for Zeke had just been the product of a very painful crush that went away as I got older and more mature.

I fooled myself with that perfectly rational explanation until a time, many years later, when I just couldn't lie to myself anymore...

Chapter 1

Zeke

The Present...

I looked at my watch impatiently for the sixteenth time in the last five minutes, and tried not to hate myself for giving in to that urge.

It was exactly eleven forty-eight a.m., and ten damn seconds.

It had been exactly fifteen seconds since I'd last checked the time. *Tick. Tock. Tick. Tock.*

"Son of a bitch!" I cursed under my breath, and scowled at the dials of the Rolex I was wearing.

Jesus, Conner. Relax. It's not like your dad's vintage Rolex Submariner is making that sound.

I let out a massive breath that I hadn't even realized I'd been holding, and put my hand back on my thigh, assuring myself I *would not* check the time...again.

Maybe my late father's cherished watch *wasn't* actually making those daunting sounds, but the action of looking at the time seemed to be the trigger that set off that unnerving noise in my head.

I'd heard it seventeen times now, every damn time I compulsively checked to see how much longer it would be until...

Shit! I had twelve damn minutes before my best friend started to saunter down the aisle on her way to the altar.

The ceremony might be...what? Twenty minutes...tops? Possibly less since it was going to be a community church type of ceremony?

Lia Harper was my best friend, and had been for approximately fourteen years now. I could manage to get through the next thirty-two minutes without doing something completely irrational, right?

I looked around the church, hoping for some kind of distraction. It was impossible *not* to notice how sparsely populated it was on the bride's side compared to the groom's side of the church.

Since Lia had no close relatives who were still living, it made sense that the only people present on her side were some of her friends.

Had it really been necessary to do the whole bride's side/groom's side thing, though? It seemed pretty ridiculous that none of the people packed like sardines on the other side of the church were willing to do overflow on Lia's side.

Apparently, Stuart's relatives and friends would rather sit on each other's laps than get comfortable on an empty bench over here.

I wasn't exactly surprised since Lia's fiancé was, quite honestly, a pretentious prick. It wasn't a shocker that Stuart's family and friends were exactly the same way.

It just pissed me off because doing things *this way* seemed like a direct snub to Lia in my eyes, and the bride-to-be could hardly avoid noticing the lopsided seating arrangement when she walked down the aisle.

Fuck! Had I known that Stuart was that insensitive to Lia's feelings, I would have found plenty of guests to fill up the empty seats on *this* side.

"Bastard," I grumbled, forcing myself not to look at my watch again, and trying to think about *anything else except* the guy my best friend was about to marry.

Nope. Don't think about that!

I was far better off just thinking about Lia, and not the jackass she was going to meet at the altar in approximately…eleven more minutes?

Don't do it, Conner! Don't look at your damn watch again. Focus, man. Just think about Lia and not the damn wedding.

I shifted positions in my seat, feeling edgy as hell as I pictured Lia's killer smile.

When she was younger, that radiant grin had always made me feel like I was her hero.

As an adult, it affected me somewhat…differently.

Oh, hell no. It was better to think about how it was with Lia when we were younger, when I'd still looked at her like she was a kid.

I tried to relax as my thoughts went back to those early, much more innocent times during my long friendship with Lia.

I'd been a senior in high school, and Lia had been a freshman the first time we'd met.

Some bastard had been trying to feel her up in the hallway next to her locker at school.

One broken nose later—his, not mine—had generated that very first smile Lia had laid on me, the one that had changed my entire world from that day forward.

I took a deep breath, and forced myself to keep my mind in the past as I swiped a bead of sweat from my forehead.

After I'd left her attacker on the hallway floor holding his bloody nose, I'd taken Lia home to her grandmother's house, and we'd been tight friends ever since.

The following year, I'd gone away to Harvard, but we'd never lost touch. We'd talked a lot on the phone, and we'd always spent as much time as possible together on my college breaks.

Our worlds had been different back then, but it had never seemed to matter.

College drama. High school drama. They were similar enough, and after all Lia had been through, she was a hell of a lot wiser than most of her high school classmates.

I released a deep breath, but I lost the fight to keep my brain focused on the past.

Dammit, how could I *not* think about Lia as an adult? The majority of the years we'd spent as best friends had been *after* she'd finished high school.

She'd grown up.

I'd tried like hell not to notice how beautiful she was once she'd crossed into womanhood, even though my dick had rarely let me forget it.

And Lia and I had remained best friends for almost a decade and a half now.

I'd forced any and all carnal thoughts about her out of my head for years, chalking up my body's reaction to her once she was an adult to rampant male hormones. I wasn't going to be that guy who lost somebody as important as Lia just because I couldn't control my dick.

Hell, I'd been a guy in my twenties, in my sexual peak. Why wouldn't my dick get hard every time I saw Lia, even if she was my best friend?

Problem was, once I'd hit my late twenties and then my thirties, my attraction to Lia had gotten worse instead of better.

It probably wasn't until I finished my law degree at Harvard, and had moved back to Seattle permanently, that I *really* knew the way I felt about Lia wasn't going to change. No matter how much I chose to live in denial.

Once we were physically in the same place, and we started doing everything together like best friends do, that damn attraction had morphed into something that was probably perilously close to… obsession.

Hell yes, *I'd* wanted to take our relationship to another level for years. Sadly, I wasn't sensing that same desire on *her* side.

Lia *had* claimed to be attracted to me…once. Too bad she'd been twenty-one years old and drunker than a skunk at the time. Even sadder, she didn't even remember that declaration the next morning. Hell, had she given me a single sign that she was attracted to me when she was in her right mind, I would have taken her up on the offer in less than a heartbeat, and gotten her naked before she could change her mind.

Unfortunately, the signal that she wanted anything other than friendship had never happened after that one, very tipsy profession. *Not once. Nothing.* And when there wasn't a single ounce of hope, what in the hell was a guy supposed to do?

She'd dated.

I'd dated, hoping to hell I'd eventually find a woman who felt as right as Lia did when we were together.

Yeah. Well. *That* had never happened.

There *had* been a time, about two years ago, that I'd gotten so frustrated that I'd finally been ready to put our friendship on the line to tell Lia the truth. I'd been ready to do almost anything to convince her that the two of us should be dating, and burning up the sheets together, instead of looking for that connection somewhere else.

It was shortly *after* I'd made that monumental decision, but before I could tell her how I felt, that Lia had met…Stuart.

As usual, my timing had totally sucked.

I clenched my fists, and let out a low curse, as I let that critical voice in my head beat the hell out of me.

Face it, Conner, it's too damn late to do anything now. You should have spoken up a long time ago, but you didn't. How damn many opportunities did you need? Lia has been an adult and single for almost a decade. And Stuart? What the fuck? It's not like you couldn't have fought for Lia when they first started dating. You knew he was a dick, and that he probably wasn't the right guy for her from the very beginning. You think you're uncomfortable right now? How are you going to feel when Stuart the dickhead is actually Lia's husband? Just remember, you're in this damn position right now because of years of denial and missed opportunities.

"Shut the fuck up!" I mumbled aloud, shutting down the internal lecture.

Yeah, so here I was, in a church, seated on the bride's side, literally waiting for the woman I loved to walk down the aisle and marry another guy. How fucked up was that?

"If it's too late, why in the hell am I even here?" I questioned myself quietly.

Dumb question, because I already knew the answer. I was *here* sweating bullets because I couldn't *not* be here for an event that was so important to Lia.

I looked around, trying desperately to find something that *felt* like Lia, some kind of sign that she'd actually had a hand in this whole lopsided fiasco of a wedding.

I scowled, my eyes narrowing as I noticed the abundance of tulips that were present on the altar, and in the flower arrangements decorating the aisle. "Tulips? Lia doesn't even like tulips. Where in the hell are the roses and daisies?" I rasped, taken aback by the fact that I couldn't find a single one of her two favorite flowers.

Hell, even the colors were all wrong.

Gold and purple sure as hell *wouldn't* have been *Lia's* preference. Had she gotten *any* say in her own damn wedding?

Son of a bitch! There wasn't one familiar thing in this whole place that stamped this event as Lia's, so I wasn't about to get the reassurance I needed to settle my ass down.

My gut already hurt, so I had no idea how I was going to get through watching Lia say her vows to the man she insisted she loved enough to marry. A guy who wasn't...me.

I'd run into Stuart enough times to know that he was a pompous asshole with a trust fund who didn't have a genuine bone in his body. We'd pretty much had a hate/hate relationship from our very first meeting.

Yeah, I'd told myself the feeling that Lia and Stuart just didn't fit was coming from a place of jealousy, but was it, really? I knew Lia as well as I knew myself. What if the lack of respect toward Lia I always sensed in Stuart *wasn't* my overactive imagination?

I squirmed on the uncomfortable bench seat. The necktie that matched my custom suit felt way too tight, but it wasn't a suit or tie that I'd never worn before. More than likely, it wasn't the damn tie that was choking me...

It was all my regrets that were strangling me to death.

I lifted my arm and looked at my watch frantically.

"Shit! It's eleven fifty-eight!" I cursed as I jerked on my tie and jumped to my feet. "And there's no fucking way I'm going to be able to hold my peace."

Tick. Tock. Tick. Tock.

"You can quit that shit, now," I grumbled. "I got it."

Hell, maybe I was slow, but I recognized that sound for exactly what it was meant to be now.

It was a goddamn warning to listen to my instincts that Lia was in trouble, and to move my ass because the window of opportunity I had to help her was closing fast.

In my gut, all jealousy aside, I just fucking *knew* that marrying Stuart *wasn't* going to make Lia happy.

Shit! Her happiness was everything to me, but it wasn't my only concern. For some reason, I also *knew* she was in some kind of… danger.

My heart was racing from the adrenaline coursing through my body, adding to the crazy sense that I had to save Lia.

I felt a few more droplets of sweat hitting my forehead as I vaulted over one of Lia's friends to get to the aisle. "Excuse me," I rumbled automatically, but didn't wait for a response.

I didn't care if my timing sucked, and it didn't matter that Lia would never see me as a possible love interest. As long as she didn't marry…*him.*

Hell, if necessary, I'd toss her beautiful ass over my shoulder and get her the hell out of here before she made the biggest mistake of her life.

Once I'd shoved my way through the closed double doors that led to the hallway outside the chapel, I stopped abruptly when I saw Lia. We were separated by the rest of the large wedding party, but my eyes instantly became laser-focused on her, like all those other people didn't even exist.

Fuck! Something's wrong!

Lia was crying, which instantly made something in my gut twist painfully.

We'd been friends for way too long for me to even briefly consider that it was a happy cry. It wasn't. I knew *her,* and her sorrow flowed from her to me in a heartbeat, just like it always did.

I pushed through the crowd around her until she saw me, and relief flooded through my body when she promptly flung herself into my arms.

Chapter 2

Lia

O
hmyGod! OhmyGod! OhmyGod! Stuart isn't here. He's
not coming to the ceremony. It's over!

I was still standing in the hallway of the church, my feet
feeling like they were rooted to the floor, and watching the retreating
figure of my fiancé's brother as he exited the building.

I hadn't said a word when he'd told me that my husband-to-be had
found a woman who was more suitable for him, and that Stuart was
backing out of the wedding.

My entire body was trembling, and I could feel the tears of confusion and relief falling down my cheeks.

I'd woken up this morning with a very heavy, sinking feeling in
the pit of my stomach that I'd tried to ignore for way too long, but
it wasn't until I'd pulled on my wedding dress in the changing room
that I'd realized I *couldn't* get married.

What had started as an inkling months ago had turned into a gut
instinct that had started to scream at me this morning.

I'd been in a full-fledged panic by the time my dress was on.

I'd been on my way to find Stuart to cancel the wedding when I'd bumped into his brother instead.

I couldn't say it wasn't painful to be totally rejected and left at the altar. The entire wedding party had been listening when Stuart's brother had calmly broken the news, and then retreated, looking like he was grateful that he'd completed a very distasteful errand.

I heard the murmured expressions of apologies from the wedding party surrounding me, but I couldn't decide exactly how I should respond.

Tears were pouring down my face, but how was I supposed to explain that the primary emotion driving all of my emotional turmoil was…relief?

Okay, there was a whole lot of confusion, anger, and sadness mixed in there somewhere, too, but I was far from *heartbroken*.

How could I even respect a man who had sent his brother to do his dirty work instead of giving me the courtesy of calling off the wedding face-to-face?

I'd just pulled the ridiculous, heavy veil that Stuart's mother had insisted on from my head when my eyes met a familiar stare.

Zeke.

His startling blue-eyed gaze never left mine as he bulldozed his way through all of the people still muttering their apologies. Mentally exhausted and broken, I vaulted into the arms of the one person who had always been there for me, sobbing out all my bewilderment and relief on his muscular, powerful shoulder as his arms wrapped around me protectively.

God, how I'd needed this man right now.

"What happened?" Zeke's gentle voice queried as my breakdown started to subside.

"Stuart is marrying somebody else," I said tearfully. "His brother just told me a few minutes ago."

And I'm perfectly fine with that.

Granted, it was humiliating to know that everybody would be talking about how Stuart had dumped the second-class woman he'd planned on marrying in favor of someone…more suitable. But those feelings were already fading away, and did I really give a damn what Stuart's friends were talking about? They'd never been my friends, too.

Honestly, I felt like I'd just dodged a bullet. I was torn between wanting to punch Stuart and wanting to thank him for finding somebody else.

"Fuck!" Zeke cursed. "Let's get the hell out of here, unless you really want to stay."

I moved back and shook my head. "I can't. Not yet. I have to tell everybody—"

"I'll take care of it, Lia. Go with Zeke." I felt a gentle touch on my arm as the soft, female voice spoke.

My friend, Ruby, had obviously heard Zeke and me talking. I shook my head. "I can't just go."

"Yes, you can," she insisted. "And you will. You don't need to make the announcement yourself. Let Zeke get you out of here, and Jett and I will let everybody know."

"She's willing to handle it, Lia. Let her," Zeke insisted.

I bit my lip for a moment before I told Ruby, "Apparently, Stuart and his mother are taking care of the reception, returning the gifts, and all the rest of the stuff that has to be done."

Ruby snorted. "It's the least he can do. You weren't the one who was sleeping with someone else, or the one who didn't even bother to show up."

I felt a painful twinge of guilt. Ruby had no idea that I wasn't exactly a heartbroken, jilted bride. Had Stuart bothered to show up, I would have cancelled the wedding myself. I just would have done it in a much nicer way than my now *ex-fiancé* had dumped me, and it wouldn't have happened because I'd been catting around with another guy.

"Say the word and we're out of here," Zeke said in an urgent tone.

"Word." My answer was automatic, since Zeke and I had been using the same lines since we were in high school. "Word. Word. Word," I added for emphasis. "Get me the hell out of here, Zeke. Please."

I really needed to escape to get my head together.

Zeke grasped my hand and pulled me into the changing area so I could gather up my things.

We were outside the church and settling into his sleek, black Range Rover moments later.

"Where to?" he rumbled as he started the engine.

"It doesn't matter. Anywhere is better than here." I trusted Zeke completely, so I was game for any place he wanted to go, as long as I was seeing the church in the rearview mirror very soon.

"My place," he decided. "Nosy people will be a lot less likely to find you there."

It was doubtful that many people would really care enough about my cancelled wedding to search me out. However, Zeke did have an incredible penthouse in a very nice neighborhood, and the security he had in his building was a lot better than mine.

"Okay," I agreed absently. "Sounds good."

I still hadn't been able to wrap my brain around the fact that the wedding I'd stressed over for the last year wasn't going to happen.

I watched as Zeke rummaged through the pockets of the suit jacket in his lap. He'd taken it off, along with his tie, before he'd entered the vehicle, and I smiled when he finally found what he was looking for. He tossed the two small packets into my lap as he drawled, "I wasn't sure if it was going to be a pear or a pineapple kind of day, so I brought both. Now that I know it's a really shitty day for you, I wish I'd brought some chocolate pudding flavor, too."

I nearly started to cry all over again. Maybe my taste in men didn't completely suck. As crappy as the entire day had been, being with Zeke made everything seem a whole lot better.

I hadn't realized that he still stayed stocked up on gourmet jelly beans for me. We'd rarely seen each other in person outside of my coffee shop during the last year or two, and lately, Zeke had been stopping by Indulgent Brews less and less, even though he was my silent partner.

"Thanks," I said gratefully as I picked up the small bag of pear Jelly Bellies and ripped them open with small smile. "Right now I'm desperate for any flavor I can get since I've been on a diet almost continually for the last year or two. I've been going through Jelly Belly withdrawals for months now."

Never once had Zeke laughed at or made fun of my gourmet jelly bean habit. If anything, he'd been my conspirator and my enabler. Maybe because he knew why I'd developed the fondness for them in the first place.

It had all started when I was twelve, and my Grandma Esther had taken me in after my parents had died suddenly in an accident.

Losing my parents at that age, and making a sudden move from rural Michigan to Seattle had both been traumatic. I hadn't really been that close to Grandma Esther when I'd first moved in with her, not because she and my dad hadn't kept in close contact, but because I just didn't see her all that often. She'd always been the faraway grandma who I loved, but rarely saw since she'd lived clear across the country.

Initially, the two of us had bonded over...jelly beans. Eventually, we'd made a game out of matching a flavor to a certain type of day or emotion.

In hindsight, I understood that my grandmother had been using the sugary treats to help me, and to figure out how I was feeling in the beginning. After that, it had just been an activity that we didn't want to end because it was entertaining. Not to mention the fact that there were very few Jelly Belly flavors that we didn't love to eat.

By the time I was fourteen, and Zeke came into my life, I'd been totally addicted to those damn jelly beans.

"Why?" Zeke growled the one-word question, pulling me away from my musings.

"Why what?" I asked as I watched him maneuver through Seattle traffic like a pro because he did it every single day.

I popped a few more jelly beans into my mouth. If there was one thing I never got tired of, it was watching Zeke Conner.

"Why in the hell were you on a diet? There's never been anything wrong with your body, Lia." He sounded confused.

I snorted. "God, I adore you for saying that, but I had to fit into this damn dress that Stuart's mother wore on her wedding day, and she was pretty thin when she got married. I still feel like the seams are going to pop at any second now. My body just isn't delicately made. I think I was born to have a curvy ass and hips, and it's really hard for me to take weight off."

"Because there's nothing there to lose," Zeke shot back. "And there's plenty of men who appreciate your curvy ass and hips. Don't you find it a little ridiculous that you had to mold yourself into a dress instead of just finding one you liked that actually fit?"

I tilted my head as I studied him. "When you put it that way, yeah, it was just a little bit sick, but Stuart was determined that I *had* to wear his mother's dress, and he wasn't overly fond of my curvy ass or my hips," I said morosely.

"Fuck Stuart!" Zeke replied tersely. "He obviously didn't have the brains to recognize or appreciate an amazing, perfect woman when he had one. The bastard never deserved you in the first place, Lia. You're better off without him. I know you're hurt and heartbroken right now, Jellybean, but give it some time. You aren't the kind of woman who is ever going to be happy to walk meekly in some guy's shadow. It's not you. The restrictions and continual expectations would have eventually crushed your spirit."

I blinked hard, and the liquid that had gathered in my tear ducts started to roll down my face. God, when had I last had anyone rush to my defense the way that Zeke always did?

Had I gotten so used to being critiqued all the time that I'd forgotten how it felt to just be…accepted?

"Shit!" Zeke cursed. "Don't cry, Lia. I promise you, everything will be okay. If it makes you feel better, I'll try not to criticize Stuart, but no guarantees I'll do a great job with that particular promise."

My tears started to fall even faster. "It's not that," I said shakily. "It's not him. It's me. I don't know what in the hell happened to me, Zeke, or how I fell into that whole trap in the first place. Maybe it was because Stuart was so wealthy and connected—"

"No. That's bullshit," Zeke interrupted. "Not all rich guys are pricks. Jesus, Lia! I'm wealthier right now than Stuart will ever be, and I've never treated you the way he did. I never would. Money isn't a golden ticket to be a complete asshole."

"Are you really richer than he is?" I asked curiously. "Stuart is a millionaire." Not that I cared, and I'd always known that Zeke wasn't exactly poor, but now I was too intrigued not to ask.

He nodded, his eyes still on the road. "I think that's one of the things I've always liked about you, Lia. We've been friends for a long time, but you've never even asked about my net worth, or how much money I have in the bank."

I shrugged. "It's never mattered. I knew you weren't poor, and that you didn't need any help in that department, so why ask?"

"I'm not a millionaire, Lia," Zeke replied stoically.

"It doesn't matter, Zeke," I rushed to assure him. "You're an extremely educated, successful guy—"

"Technically," he interrupted, "since my assets exceed a billion dollars, I'm a billionaire."

Chapter 3

Zeke

There was no real reason *why* I'd never told Lia exactly how much money I had.

Like she'd said, she never asked, and it had never been that important to either one of us. But holy hell, the moment Lia had mentioned *Stuart's* wealth, I'd almost fucking lost it.

Suddenly, I'd wanted her to know that if she really wanted to marry a guy who had a lot of money, I was her man.

Yeah, that instinct was totally ridiculous because I knew damn well that Lia wouldn't hesitate to marry a guy who was dirt poor if she really loved him. So I had no idea what that whole chest-beating, I'm-richer-than-the-idiot-you-were-going-to-marry bullshit was all about.

"How did I not know that my best friend was a billionaire?" Lia asked softly. "I didn't think there was very much we didn't know about each other."

"Now that you do, is it going to make any difference?" I asked.

"No," she answered in a contemplative tone. "Wait! Maybe it will, a little. I might not feel quite so guilty or argue as much about you picking up the tab whenever we go to a pricey restaurant."

I grinned. "I always told you I could afford it, Jellybean."

She snorted. "I guess I never realized that paying wasn't even going to put a small dent in your bank account. But that still doesn't mean that you *always* get to pay."

I chuckled. If I'd expected my net worth to impress her, I would have been sorely disappointed right now. "So do you understand that money doesn't make every guy a jerk? You already know billionaires, Lia. Look at Jett Lawson, Ruby's fiancé, and all of his brothers. Jett treats Ruby like she's the most important thing in his universe, which I'm pretty sure she is, and the Lawson brothers have some of the highest net worths in the world."

"I know," Lia said with a small groan. "Jett adores Ruby, and he acts like he can't live without her. If she wasn't my friend, and I didn't know how much she deserves a guy like that, I'd probably be green with envy."

"So if Ruby wasn't with him, you might be interested in Jett?" I prodded.

Oh, way to go, Conner. Lia hasn't even gotten out of her wedding dress yet, and you're already worried about who the next guy might be.

Lia let out a startled laugh. "No, that's not why I'd be jealous. It's not the guy. It's their relationship. Nothing against Jett, mind you, but I can't quite see those two with anyone else *except* each other. They love each other so much that I'm pretty sure they were meant to be together." She paused before she added, "I really don't know what it would be like to have a guy look at me the way Jett looks at Ruby. I don't think *any* guy has ever looked at me like that." She took a deep breath. "I guess Stuart was just…different."

"A pretentious prick, you mean?" I asked before I could stop myself. "It wasn't the money, Lia. It was the lifestyle. The snobby private schools, the trust funds, the country clubs, and the whole idea that money gives a person some kind of superiority. If you hang around with an entire crowd who believes that shit, you end up caught up in that theory, and it rules your life. Everyone is trying so hard to outdo each other that appearances become their biggest priority. It's pretty twisted."

She was silent for a moment before she said, "Maybe I got caught up in that world, too, at least for a little while."

I shook my head. "Not for the same reasons. I think you just wanted to fit in."

"I felt like Stuart's love was conditional, and if I wanted him to love me more, I had to be the woman he needed," she replied with a sigh. "It wasn't like that in the beginning, but things changed."

"You can hate me for saying this," I told her huskily. "But I'm pretty damn glad he met somebody else."

"Me, too," she answered quietly. "I'm not exactly naïve, but I had no idea he was cheating on me. I guess I was so busy at the store, and with getting that crazy wedding together, that I never noticed any of the signs."

"Don't beat yourself up about that, Lia," I warned. "That was his issue. It wasn't your responsibility to notice any of the signals. The bastard should have kept his dick in his pants."

"I don't even know what she looks like or who she is," Lia pondered.

"Doesn't matter," I reassured her. "There isn't another woman in the world who's as beautiful as you are, Lia."

"Maybe she has a skinnier ass," she joked halfheartedly.

"Then she'd definitely be a lot less attractive than you are, Jellybean," I retorted.

If any guy didn't lust after a woman with a body like Lia's, there was something wrong with him. She was built like a damn goddess, and her curvy ass and rounded hips were definitely an asset, not a deficit.

She laughed as she tossed back a few more jelly beans. "If you keep feeding me Jelly Bellies like this, I'll gain back the weight I lost in a couple of days."

"Good," I said happily. "I have a pretty large stash at my place. That will help."

She sighed. "You have to adore a best friend who doesn't care if your ass is too big."

"Any time you have to practically starve to maintain a certain weight, you're too damn skinny," I grumbled. "I used to keep you well supplied with jelly beans every single day, and your ass looked just fine."

"Says the man who has never seen me naked," she teased.

I nearly swallowed my tongue. She had no fucking idea how badly I really did want to get her naked, and that I sure as hell wouldn't be disappointed if I got that wish. "Feel free to take your clothes off anytime, and I'll still tell you that you're fucking perfect," I answered, trying to keep my tone lighthearted, even though I had visions of a nude Lia dancing in my damn head.

"Please," she drawled. "I'm your best friend, and probably the last woman you want to see naked."

Hell, if she only knew! Honestly, she was the *only* female I wanted to get naked.

Lia was quiet for a few seconds before she asked, "So are you going to tell me how you ended up a billionaire? I knew your mom and dad were well-off, but I had no idea they were quite *that* wealthy."

"So you think a guy like me must have inherited all my money from my parents?" I said in a pseudo-offended tone.

"Stop stalling. You know that's not what I think. Tell me."

I shrugged. "You already know that I did a duel degree at Harvard, so I came out of school with a law degree and an MBA. Law was my passion, and investment analysis was more of a hobby until I lost my dad." I stopped to clear my throat. Even though it had been several years, the wound of losing my father still felt pretty damn fresh. We'd only worked together in his law firm for a short time before I'd had to take over after his death. "After Mom retained more money than she could spend in several lifetimes, I did inherit several million dollars, and one of the best law firms in the country, when Dad died. So I started investing, and some of those companies I bought into early are enormous corporations now. My law firm does well, so I never really stopped investing. I guess you could say that I did inherit some of my money, but not the majority of it."

"God, you're an amazing man, Zeke Conner," Lia said, sounding slightly awed. "You already had enough on your plate when you were taking over the firm. I don't know where you found the time to manage a large portfolio."

It was funny how much a guy could get accomplished when he had no life. Yeah, I'd dated. Occasionally. I'd even had a few girlfriends. But for the most part, my personal life was fairly uneventful. "It wasn't really all that difficult," I answered.

"Don't do that," Lia scolded. "I hate it when you do that. Don't downplay the fact that you've accomplished something that very few people could do. You've always been the smartest and most driven person I know, and I don't like it when you don't take enough credit for some of the amazing things you do."

"So you'd rather have a best friend who's a blowhard?"

"Like that's ever going to happen?" Lia asked drolly. "You're the most humble person I've ever met. I doubt you're going to turn into a braggart tomorrow if you toot your own horn occasionally."

"Completely unnecessary. I have you to do that for me," I teased.

Lia rarely missed an opportunity to brag on my behalf. I never had to say a word. I hadn't lacked for effusive praise and support from Lia over the years. She'd tell me, and anyone else who would listen, every single reason why I was such a great guy.

She let out an exasperated huff. "Someone needs to do it," she replied defensively. "And is it really that bad having somebody who's so proud of you that they can't stop talking about you?"

Hell, no. It wasn't bad at all. Lia's willingness to notice all the good things about a person, and easily forgive the bad, was one of her most endearing qualities. "Not at all," I assured her. "I just hope I've been half as supportive of you as you've been with me over the years."

She snorted. "Zeke, you helped me get Indulgent Brews by being my silent partner in that coffee shop. I wouldn't have a successful store of my own if it wasn't for you. You've help me through every challenge, disappointment, and difficult event I've ever had in my life since I was a freshman in high school. You're the one who's with me right now, after getting dumped at the altar by a man who was cheating on me for God only knows how long during our engagement. So yeah, I think you've been plenty supportive."

I drummed my fingers on the steering wheel as we inched forward on an extremely busy street. "I have to tell you something, Lia, and it might piss you off."

"Just tell me," she said encouragingly.

"When I saw you in the hallway at the church, I had every intention of stopping the whole damn wedding. I don't know why it took me so long, but I had a gut instinct I couldn't ignore. I knew you weren't going to be happy with Stuart, and just hauling you out of that church, whether you wanted to go or not, wasn't an option that was completely off the table, either. I can't explain what really happened at the church earlier, but I was terrified you were making a huge mistake. Hell, somehow I actually *knew* you were."

A minute ticked by, and then two.

I was getting nervous when she finally answered. "I'm not pissed off. You were right. Marrying Stuart would have been the biggest mistake of my life. I have a confession of my own."

"What?"

She sighed. "I was looking for Stuart when I ran into his brother. I was going to call off the wedding myself. Stuart just saved me the trouble by being a cheating bastard who couldn't keep his dick in his pants. The ceremony wasn't going to happen, Zeke. I was a wreck this morning, but by the time I had this stupid dress on, I was completely freaked out because I knew I couldn't go through with it. Your intuition was right. Maybe you were picking up on *my* panic. I don't know why it took a whole year for all those warning bells to go off for me, but I'm not heartbroken that this wedding never happened."

I was momentarily stunned. She never planned to walk down that aisle today? "So you aren't in love with Stuart anymore?" I questioned cautiously.

"No," she confirmed in a sad tone. "I don't know if I was ever in love with him. I think I'm still trying to figure all that out. I just spent over a year turning myself inside out to try to be the woman he wanted to marry, and I don't even understand why."

She sounded so lost and confused that I reached out and took her hand in mine. "We'll figure it out together, Lia. Maybe your heart isn't broken, but the bastard did mess with your head. You were still reeling from Esther's death when you met Stuart. You were vulnerable. Don't blame yourself."

Hell, she could blame me instead. I should have been there for her, but I wasn't. I'd been too busy feeling sorry for myself because she'd seemed happy with another guy.

She nodded and squeezed my hand. "I need to find myself again, Zeke. I'm not even sure I know who I am anymore."

Fuck! I hated the exposed defenselessness in her tone.

I'd walked away from this woman once when I should have stuck to her like glue because she'd been unguarded and grieving.

That was never going to happen again.

"You're still the same Lia Harper," I informed her. "Gorgeous, fearless, blonde bombshell with the shapeliest ass on the planet. A connoisseur of coffee, and a lover of jelly beans. You're the kindest, bravest person I've ever known. You talk about my accomplishments? You're not even twenty-eight years old yet, Lia, and you already own a very successful business that you're working on expanding for an even greater success. None of those things ever changed. All you need is some time to make yourself a priority again, and I'm going to be right here to make sure that you do."

I heard her head flop back against the headrest as she said, "God, I missed you so much, Zeke. I know we talk, and we see each other at the shop, but we were never the same after Stuart came into the picture. What happened to us?"

I wasn't even going to pretend that I didn't know what she was talking about. I knew what it was like to miss Lia with every fiber of my being. "It wasn't your fault," I said huskily. "I hated Stuart's guts, so I was the one who stepped back when I should have been there for you. I never thought the bastard was good enough for you, but I wanted you to be happy. I thought you were, even though I felt like the two of you never quite...fit. It always seemed like you were the only one who compromised, but I'm starting to think you did a hell of a lot more than just cater to his needs. I should have been paying more attention. I'm sorry I wasn't there when you needed someone to be looking out for your best interests, Jellybean."

"You're my best friend, Zeke, not my father," she said drily. "It wasn't your responsibility to recognize my dysfunctional relationship. And I stepped back, too. I knew you didn't like Stuart, but I think I was so caught up in that relationship that I'm not sure I would have listened to any of your objections when I wasn't being rational myself. I'm a big girl, Zeke. I made some bad choices, and that's on me." She took a deep breath before she added, "But I'm so damn grateful that you're here to help me figure everything out."

"I'm not going anywhere, Lia. We have all the time in the world to figure it out."

Maybe she didn't know it yet, but if things went my way, when all of this was over, she'd be mine, and I'd make damn sure that nobody ever hurt her again.

Chapter 4

Lia

Zeke had made a few detours on the way back to his penthouse, and one of those errands had been to pick up food from our favorite Chinese place. We were both foodies, but we hadn't shared a meal from our favorite spots in a long time.

I'd changed out of my dress and into a pair of jeans and a loose, tie-dyed shirt, clothing that I'd left over at Zeke's place a long time ago. My jeans fit a lot looser since I'd dropped some weight, but I didn't care because I was comfortable, and I felt a little more like myself again.

He'd changed into a pair of jeans, too, and a button-down baby-blue shirt that made his eyes look even bluer than normal.

The TV was on low in the background as we ate, but I was pretty sure neither one of us was paying attention to the news as we relaxed in Zeke's living room.

I finally dropped my fork on my plate and reached for the glass of white wine he'd poured me before he'd seated himself on the couch. I took a long sip and swallowed before I said, "I don't know what

I'm going to do about my grandma's will. If I'm not married by my birthday, I'm screwed."

I'd loved the grandparent who had raised me like her own after my parents had died, but I still didn't get why she'd put the condition in her will that I couldn't inherit unless I was married before my twenty-eighth birthday. If I didn't meet that condition, everything went to distant relatives we'd never even met, and charities she supported.

Not that Grandma Esther *owed* me anything. She'd raised me when nobody else would have taken me in. But it stung more than a little that, in some ways, she'd been trying to change me, too.

Nevertheless, since I'd *planned* on being married by my birthday, the condition had never really made all that much difference. It had just halted my ability to inherit until Stuart and I were married.

"I reviewed all the documents like you asked me to do after Esther passed away," Zeke answered. "The estate attorney is right. If challenged, you could very well lose. It was written so well that it could be upheld by a judge. I have no idea what she was thinking when she wrote it, Lia, but you know damn well that she loved you like a daughter, and she'd want everything she had to go to you."

Zeke's expression was grim, but I didn't doubt his opinion since my best friend was a high-powered defense attorney. Even though he didn't specialize in wills and trusts, Zeke was a Harvard Law graduate, and he had a good grasp on what could be challenged according to the law.

"Unfortunately, I don't exactly have time to find another groom," I said wistfully. I was turning twenty-eight in exactly one week from today. "I can deal with losing the monetary assets, but it's going to kill me to see all of the things that have so much sentimental value go, too, since she included everything in her estate. I'll have to up my installment payments to you."

I felt like a failure because I couldn't pay off the money I owed to him. I'd planned on buying Zeke out of my shop completely once my grandma's estate had gotten settled, and then putting the rest of the money into starting a second store. I knew damn well that our agreement had been more of a favor from him, even though he'd claimed he was making a good investment. "I don't know how else to get you bought out. And the second Indulgent Brews will have to wait."

"I don't want the damn money, and I would have never agreed to take a penny from you in installments if you hadn't threatened to cut my balls off if I didn't take it," Zeke answered grumpily. "We agreed that I'd be your silent partner when you refused to just take the money as a gift from a friend, and that you could buy me out at any time. There was no time limit, and I've told you about a million times that I'd much rather you reinvest the money you insist on paying me every month back into growing the business. You'd have a second shop by now if you weren't so damn bullheaded."

The argument was a familiar one. Zeke had wanted to just give me all the funds I'd needed for my startup as a gift, and I'd adamantly refused. What kind of friend would take advantage of another friend that way? I wasn't about to agree to something like that when there was no ownership in it for him to guarantee that money. So our silent partnership had gotten drafted and signed. "You didn't want to be a partner," I reminded him. "You did it strictly to help me."

The fact that he'd shared that he was a billionaire before he'd even hit the age of thirty-two didn't make one iota of difference to me.

"Knowing you don't need that money doesn't make me feel any better about the fact that I can't pay you back in full in a few weeks. I want to know I've earned that store, and you're my best friend, Zeke," I said remorsefully.

"If you feel that bad, you could just marry me," he suggested matter-of-factly. "You'd inherit because you'd be married before your birthday, and you wouldn't feel like you had to hold off on a second store. Problem solved."

I started to laugh, but then halted abruptly as I looked at him on the couch from my seat in a comfy recliner.

He was staring at me with a familiar look. An expression that had none of his usual humor or teasing.

Holy shit! He's...serious.

I set my empty wine glass on the side table and folded my arms in front of me. "I'm pretty sure Angelique wouldn't be happy," I said in an easy tone. "God, Zeke, I appreciate how willing you are to help me out, but you obviously haven't thought this whole idea through yet."

He shrugged his massive shoulders. "We broke up, not that we were ever really a couple in the first place. We just dated for a while. I haven't seen her in months. Where have you been?"

Where have I been?

I'd been so busy with my business, and preparing for my wedding, that I'd obviously failed to notice that Zeke didn't have the gorgeous brunette on his arm anymore.

"I'm sorry," I answered, feeling like a shit because I hadn't known that Zeke was flying solo. Had she broken it off, or had he done it? Had she hurt him? Was he bummed out because he wasn't seeing her anymore?

"Don't be sorry. It was never serious."

I sighed as I leaned back into the comfortable chair. "Who broke it off?" I asked curiously.

"Mutual agreement," he replied. "I think she was interested in dating, and eventually marrying, a guy with money more than she was into me, personally. Neither one of us were heartbroken over it. We just weren't looking for the same thing."

God, I hated the fact that no woman had ever really looked past Zeke's eligibility, or the fact that he was a high-powered attorney who owned one of the best defense firms in the country.

Why hadn't some lucky woman snapped him up just because he was an incredible guy, and one of the kindest, most generous people on Earth?

Sure, women found him physically attractive. I mean, who *wouldn't?*

It had certainly *never* escaped my notice that Zeke was smoking hot. It still didn't. I'd just tried to ignore it for the good of our friendship after he'd set me straight on my twenty-first birthday.

Strangely, I felt more than one twinge of uneasiness at the thought of Zeke pledging his life to a woman. I'd never really thought about what our relationship would look like if he wasn't single, maybe because he never seemed to get serious with any woman for any length of time. Not that I blamed Zeke, since he'd never found a woman who really saw...him.

He looked up and pinned my gaze with his. "I think I just offered to marry you. Does that mean you're refusing?"

The timbre of his voice sent an electric zing down my spine. I wasn't immune to the dangerous, wickedly low tone of his voice. I just wanted to pretend that it didn't make every female hormone in my body stand up and take notice. "You weren't serious."

"I was completely serious, Lia. You need to get married. I'm available. No offense, but I think I'm a better option than Stuart. I wouldn't change a hair on your head, much less try to make you into someone you're not. I happen to think you're absolutely incredible the way you've always been."

Oh, *sweet Jesus*, I *knew* that intense, determined, stubborn expression on his face right now. I just hadn't seen it in a very long time. "You can't just marry me," I protested. "I adore you for offering, but the whole idea is...just crazy."

Problem was, I knew Ezekiel Conner was far from insane.

He was funny.

He was sweet when he wanted to be.

He oozed a masculine sex appeal that most women couldn't ignore.

He was wealthy.

He was highly educated, ridiculously intelligent, and extremely successful.

But...he was just *my friend*.

Women like *me* did not marry men like Zeke Conner.

He was way too...perfect.

"Think about it, Lia," Zeke said calmly. "You deserve to open another store, and to get out from under the expenses you acquired from the first one. You don't want to accept the money I gave you as a gift, so that means you feel like you have to pay it back before you can keep moving forward. If you marry me, you don't have to commit to forever. There's nothing in the will that requires you to *stay* married. You meet the terms, collect your inheritance, and then we can get a divorce if that's what you really want."

I gaped at him. "Isn't that what you'd want, too? I don't get it. What do *you* get from this? I know you'd do anything for me as a friend, but don't you think you're going a little too far?"

I chewed on a fingernail nervously as my eyes stayed still fixed on his.

"Do you really want to know?" he asked huskily.

I nodded slowly.

"I get the chance to talk you into my bed for as long as it takes to get your inheritance," he answered with what sounded like a bluntly honest tone.

"Why would you want *that*?" I squeaked.

I'd offered myself up to him once, and I'd regretted it ever since.

Zeke had been my friend for fourteen years, and there had never been a single mention of anything more than friendship between the two of us except for my drunken confession on my twenty-first birthday.

"Do you really think that I haven't noticed that you grew into a beautiful woman? You've had the power to get my dick hard for years now, Lia. In fact, it's hard to believe you never noticed," he drawled.

"You've never wanted to screw me," I challenged.

"Sure I did," he said with a smirk. "What red-blooded man wouldn't?"

"Tons of them," I said nervously.

All of my ex-boyfriends, at least.

"I did, and still do, want to fuck you," he said as he folded his muscular arms across his chest. "I've just never talked about it. I wasn't sensing the interest on your side, my timing has always sucked, and I didn't want my dick to ruin a good friendship. But had you so much as crooked your finger at me, I would have had you in my bed before you could have changed your mind. Marry me, Lia. I'm never going to force you to do anything you don't want, but at least give me a fucking chance to show you that we'd be just as good at being lovers as we have been at being friends. If you decide that's not what you want, we'll get a divorce."

His expression was stoic, and his beautiful blue eyes were shuttered. For the first time in our very long friendship, I had absolutely no idea what he was thinking.

This man wasn't the Zeke I knew, but he was still familiar. I felt like I was in some kind of weird dream, and seeing a side of my best friend that I'd never noticed before.

But he's still my Zeke.

I *did* start thinking about his offer. Maybe it hadn't been the most romantic proposal in the world, but just the fact that he'd be willing to sacrifice his freedom, even temporarily, to help me achieve my own goals, made me start to cry.

Not that I was really buying the crap about him lusting after my body. It was obviously his way of pretending he'd get something out of the deal if I said *yes.*

However, I desperately wanted to pay him back for everything he'd done since I'd opened my successful coffee shop. And the only way I was going to be able to do that was to get my inheritance.

He'd trusted me completely when he'd readily forked over that huge sum of money.

Not only had Zeke given me the money to start Indulgent Brews generously, but he'd been there for me every step of the way while it was growing as well. He called himself a silent partner, but he'd been around when shit had hit the fan, too. I'd shared my knowledge of coffee with him, and he'd taught me everything I knew about being a good businesswoman.

"Okay," I said softly, my decision made.

He lifted a brow. "Okay…what?"

"I'll marry you. But don't think for a single second that I believe that you've ever lusted after my body. But I'll make sure this temporary sacrifice is worth it to you somehow. I know you definitely don't need the money, but I'll figure something out."

"But you're open to letting me convince you otherwise?" he asked.

I snorted. "Yeah. Okay. I agree."

I was fine with keeping up the pretense that he wanted me if it made *him* feel better. But I knew he was simply doing me a favor—again.

He grinned at me, and I smiled back at him through my tears because it was a mischievous smile I hadn't seen in a long time. I swiped the remaining tears from my face as I said, "I'm not even sure how to thank you this time, Zeke, but I'll think of something."

"All I've ever really wanted was a chance with you, so don't thank me. I'm getting exactly what I want," he replied hoarsely.

My heart tripped, his sexy baritone affecting me in a way I'd never noticed before.

This is all temporary. Don't start thinking it's anything more than a friend helping a friend in a very overboard, insane kind of way.

I released a tremulous breath. I definitely wasn't immune to any of Zeke's masculine charms and assets, so I could only hope he didn't push the whole attempted seduction ruse too far.

If he did, I wasn't so sure I wouldn't have him naked before he could back off.

Chapter 5

Zeke

"She didn't even believe me when I said I wanted her," I muttered unhappily to my friend, billionaire tech mogul, Jett Lawson.

Jett's fiancée, Ruby, had already left Jett's penthouse with Lia. The moment Lia had told Ruby that she needed to plan a second wedding in a hurry, the two of them had hightailed it out of the building to go find a dress.

"Then you'll just have to convince her it's true," Jett answered. "Where is the honeymoon?"

"I haven't really thought about that," I said, annoyed with myself that the honeymoon hadn't even entered my mind yet. Then again, she'd just agree to marry me yesterday.

I'd been too damn focused on the fact that Lia was going to be mine. To hell with the "temporary" shit. I had to find a way to convince her that we belonged together.

Jett raised a brow. "Since this wedding is going to occur in record time, I suggest you figure it out. Both of you could use the break, and Seattle in the winter isn't exactly romantic. Lia trained up a manager for the store, and Ruby is there almost every day to deliver her baked goods to the store. We can watch the shop."

I grimaced as I informed him, "Stuart was taking her to Dubai."

"On their honeymoon?" Jett questioned, his face incredulous. "That's even more depressing than Seattle in the winter. I'm not saying it isn't an interesting place to visit, but I doubt the UAE is on the top of most women's romantic honeymoon wish list destinations."

"He apparently has some business interests there, and wanted to drum up a few more," I grumbled.

"Asshole," Jett said irritably.

I nodded. "Definitely."

"You should take her someplace warm and tropical. Hell, I'm no expert on women, but there are a lot more romantic places to go in the world than Dubai," Jett rumbled.

"Bora Bora?" I considered.

Jett shook his head. "You'll hit the rainy season this time of year."

I shrugged. "So we'll end up shacked up together in an overwater bungalow."

"Stop thinking with your dick," Jett insisted. "You can't have sex every minute of your honeymoon. You're trying to win her over, not wear her out."

Since there were no guarantees she'd even end up in my bed, I did need a location where we could just relax and have fun.

"Hawaii?" I pondered.

Jett shook his head. "Uninspired. Everybody goes there on their honeymoon. It's fun, but the food is nothing to get excited about."

"The Bahamas?"

"Boring," Jett scoffed.

"Cancun?" I growled, getting annoyed.

"Better," he said with a satisfied nod. "It's really nice there in the fall and winter, and I know Lia really likes Mexican food. Just a suggestion, but I'd go for Playa del Carmen."

I'd been to both Cancun and Playa. They were close to each other, but Jett was right. Playa was a little quieter, but still didn't lack for things to do.

"I'll get the trip planned," I agreed.

"She'll love it," Jett replied supportively, like he hadn't just told me that I was uninspired.

"I'll need to get moving on those arrangements. Lia's twenty-eighth birthday is Saturday, so the wedding is happening late afternoon on Friday," I informed him.

Jett nodded slowly. "Yeah, Ruby told me about the will requirements. It's kind of strange. Was her grandmother in her right mind when she did it?"

I let out a bark of laughter. "You didn't know Esther," I informed him. "She was as sharp as a tack until the day she died. I don't completely get it, either. She adored Lia. I don't understand why she made *any* rules for the inheritance. And there's nothing that says that Lia has to stay married for any length of time. She just wanted her...married. Not like Esther at all."

"So the terms are easy to fulfill?"

"Very," I informed him. "Lia asked me to look over every document, and I have. I'm not an expert in wills and trusts, but it was pretty straightforward."

"Do you think Lia felt like she had to marry Stuart because of the terms of the will?"

I frowned at Jett and shook my head. "No. She doesn't care about giving up the money—other than the fact that she wouldn't be able to buy me out of our partnership right away. The stuff in the estate that has sentimental value to her is a little different, but I don't think she felt pressed to marry Stuart at all. I think she convinced herself that she loved him, and that he was her perfect partner. I have no fucking idea why."

"Is she okay?" he asked in a serious tone. "I mean, she didn't really look terribly broken up earlier, but it could all be an act."

It felt way too personal to share Lia's confession that she'd intended to call off the wedding herself, so I didn't.

"She'll be fine," I answered simply. "I'll make sure that she is."

"I think you should tell her how you feel, Zeke," Jett insisted. "Keeping your mouth shut hasn't exactly gotten you anywhere."

"Yeah," I admitted. "I came to that same conclusion myself after I sat down in the chapel yesterday. I tried to tell her when we got back to my place last night, but like I said, she thinks I'm just making up a reason to help her. I swear, she has some strange idea in her head that makes her think it's *impossible* for me to be attracted to her that way."

Jett rose from the couch, and I followed him into the kitchen. I gratefully took a second bottle of beer, and sucked down half of it as we both leaned against the counter.

He took a gulp from his own bottle before he said, "Make her listen, Zeke. Put your heart on the line. It sounds like those feelings have been there for you for a long time. You can correct me if I'm wrong, but I don't think this is all about a simple physical attraction. It's pretty damn obvious that you care about her."

I nodded. I was done trying to bullshit myself. "I'm in love with her. Probably have been for a long time. I can't really pinpoint the exact moment that everything changed for me. Hell, I've loved Lia in one way or another since the day we met. I'm not even sure if the attraction came first once we were both adults, or if I was already in love with her by then. All I really know is that I finally have the opportunity I've always wanted to try to convince her that we were never meant to be *just friends* all our lives, and I don't want to fuck it up."

"Has it ever occurred to you that Lia could be in denial, too?" Jett questioned.

I shot him a doubtful look. "Not really. I've never seen a single sign that she wants to be more than friends." That drunken birthday confession sure as hell didn't count. "Believe me, I've watched for any kind of signal from her for years that she might be willing to take our friendship to a different level."

He shrugged. "There's denial, and then there's *complete denial*. In your case, those feelings weren't all that far from the surface most of the time. You could deny your attraction just enough that you never acted on those emotions. In her case, what if those feelings are buried so deep she doesn't even know that they exist right now?

It's just a theory, but I know Lia adores you. Even when you're not around, she's talking about you. I think she mentions you in a single conversation a lot more than she's ever brought up Stuart. I've seen you two together, Zeke. Maybe you're not a romantic couple, but your dynamics are very similar, minus any of the touchy-feely stuff. I could be wrong, but in my mind, the feelings are there on both sides. She's just learned to bury it a lot deeper than you do."

"If that's true, how in the hell did she end up with Stuart?" I growled.

"That's your question to ask, not mine," he answered calmly. "But it isn't like you've never seen anyone else. If she's under the assumption that the two of you could never be more than friends, don't you think it makes sense that she'd be looking elsewhere? Maybe she picked the wrong guy, but you can't blame her for searching. No matter how cynical we get, I don't think anybody ever completely loses hope that the right person is out there somewhere. Even if we don't admit it to ourselves."

I shot him a questioning look. "Why do I have a feeling you're talking from personal experience?"

"Because I am," Jett admitted freely. "Love was the last thing I was hoping for when I met Ruby. I was scarred inside and out, and let's face it, my activities are limited because of my bum leg. I'd already been dumped by one woman because I couldn't do some of the things a normal guy my age could do. Having any woman fall in love with me was an impossibility to me back then, unless it was an act just to get to my money. I wasn't expecting a woman like Ruby, and I sure as hell didn't know that she'd find that tiny spark of hope that I didn't even know existed. I'm still not sure exactly how it happened, but Ruby managed to find that well-buried, microscopic particle that still wanted to believe that a woman could love me like she does." He grinned. "Once she did, it was all over for me, my friend."

I was quiet for a moment. I'd never heard this part of Jett and Ruby's romance. Yeah, Jett had a noticeable limp, but it never seemed to slow him down all that much. "You don't look like a guy who's exactly sad about that fate."

"I'm not," he said, his smile growing even wider. "I guess my whole point is that we don't always know what we want until we get it. I think if you could manage to find that part of Lia that wants you to love her, and she knows you're there to love her back, it might change everything for both of you. If nothing else, at least you'll be able to say you tried."

"Failure really is not an option," I said gruffly.

I had no idea if there was a part of Lia that wanted me to love her, but I could sure as hell look.

"Then don't fail," he suggested.

"I don't intend to," I confirmed.

I'd already come to terms with the fact that it was Lia or no one for me, so I was going to be a guy who was literally fighting for his life, and I wasn't planning on giving up.

Chapter 6

Lia

"**W**hat in the hell am I doing?" I asked my friend, Ruby, in a moment of panic.

It hadn't even been a full week since Stuart had left me at the church alone, and now I was just about ready to walk down the aisle again, with my best friend this time.

I had no idea how we'd managed to pull this whole thing together in less than a week, but I'd forever be grateful to Ruby, and to Zeke's mother, Marlene.

Zeke's mom had been elated when she learned that her son and I were getting married, and she'd taken the whole last-minute wedding thing in stride. If I didn't already think she was an amazing woman—which I did—I'd at least be totally in awe of her organizational skills.

Zeke and I were getting hitched in a century-old chapel in Gig Harbor, a lovely town about an hour from Seattle, and the reception was taking place at the yacht club nearby.

Everything had come together perfectly, but the fact that I was actually marrying Zeke was still…surreal.

"You're getting married to the right man this time," Ruby answered as she smoothed down the skirt of my second wedding dress. "And you look gorgeous."

I had to admit that I felt good as I looked at my reflection in the mirror. I felt...like me.

"It's a really nice dress," I said as I looked at the deceptively simple, long-sleeved, ivory gown. My choice had been a style that cinched at the waist, and fell in curtains of silk and lace to my feet.

When I caught Ruby's reflection in the mirror as she flitted around to arrange my dress, I added, "You look gorgeous, too."

Ruby stood up straight next to me in her rose silk gown. "I feel like a princess," she said breathlessly.

I shot her a tremulous smile. Oh, God. I really hoped I was doing the right thing. "I just feel so guilty," I confessed. "You know this is all a ruse, but Marlene doesn't. And she's so happy."

"Does it feel right?" Ruby asked as she fussed with the silver clips that were holding my curly blonde hair back from my face.

I'd decided to go without a veil since it was more my style.

"Strangely, it doesn't feel wrong," I told her. "I know that sounds weird, but I trust Zeke. I always have."

"Then roll with it," Ruby replied. "And stop feeling guilty. Zeke really wants this, and I think deep down inside, you do, too. I know you think this isn't real, but there's a marriage license that says differently. I think you'll be happy together, Lia."

"You say that like you think Zeke and I will stay married," I answered.

Ruby shrugged. "Who says you won't? Maybe you'll eventually figure out that Zeke is the right guy for you. I think he always has been, but you just never noticed."

"Zeke and me?" I squeaked. "That's crazy. We've always been just friends. Guys like Zeke don't marry women like me."

Ruby gave me a disbelieving look. "Why wouldn't they?"

"He's rich, and he's obscenely hot. Not to mention highly educated. He did the duel major at Harvard, for God's sake. I graduated from high school, went to work at a coffee shop, and took part-time classes at a local college until I finally got an associate's degree. Zeke is in control of one of the most prestigious law firms in the country. I'm not even remotely the woman for someone like him."

Ruby pulled a face. "Please. Don't start talking about a guy being out of your league. I'm a homeless woman who just got engaged to one of the richest men in the world. Sometimes those superficial things just don't matter. It's what's in here that counts." She thumped a hand on her chest.

She was right. "But you know we're just friends."

Ruby rolled her eyes. "Zeke has always looked at you like you were the only female who existed. If he looked at you as a friend, it was a long time ago. The guy adores you. It's pretty obvious. Are you saying that you've never seen him as an attractive guy?"

"I did. I do. I just never thought about…him being mine. I admit, I was infatuated with him when I was younger, but even then, I wasn't thinking he'd ever *marry me*."

Ruby let out a playful laugh. "Well, you better consider it, because you're about to walk down the aisle, and your groom looks a hell of a lot like Zeke Conner."

"But you know it's not for real." Zeke was doing all of this for me, and I shuddered as I thought about just how much he was giving up to do this whole charade.

He'd flat out refused to do a prenup, no matter how many times I'd stomped my foot about it, stating that he trusted me over and over again. Not that I didn't appreciate his trust, but the guy had a hell of a lot of assets at stake in this whole arrangement. Since my only plan was to pay him back and not rip him off, I'd finally let it go. It was one of those rare times when I knew he wasn't going to compromise.

"We'll see whether it's real or not," Ruby said cheerfully. "You've obviously never seen the way he looks at you. Try paying attention. You might find out you like it."

Ruby never stopped smiling as she took my hand and led me the short distance to the chapel.

After handing me my flowers, she did her own walk down the aisle until she was standing across from Jett and Zeke.

I froze as I looked down the aisle. It was a sweet, cozy chapel, but that short aisle seemed like it was miles long. As I looked around the small venue at the family and friends who had come to see Zeke and I get married, I suddenly realized the gravity of my decision.

Oh God, I can't do this to my best friend.

I know he cares about me, but I can't make him marry me just to get my inheritance.

All of his family is here, and they think all of this is…real.

I have to stop this right now.

It was like déjà vu.

Except I wouldn't be calling the wedding off for *me* this time. I'd be doing it for *Zeke*.

I'd gotten so caught up in doing tasks that had to be done over the last few days that I'd failed to think about how *really* unfair this all was to Zeke. Maybe because *he* kept telling me that it was no big deal.

But it was a *very big deal.*

I looked up, and I met Zeke's beautiful blue eyes across the small room. His gaze was steady and reassuring, but I couldn't shake the guilt that was pummeling me.

I didn't move. I felt like I was literally frozen in place.

Zeke never broke eye contact as he stepped down from the platform, and strode down the aisle until he was at my side.

"You look absolutely gorgeous, and you're not backing out," he said roughly in my ear as he took my hand. "Don't even think about it."

I wasn't surprised that he knew exactly how I was feeling. He usually did.

"I'm sorry. I can't do this," I whispered loud enough so that he could hear. "It's just not right. I should have never said *yes.* Everyone here thinks all this is real except for Ruby and Jett."

"We're going to walk down this aisle together. Come on, Lia. We've always made it through everything together. And this is no different. Walk with me. You look stunningly beautiful, and my family is here. This is real for me. Please don't make me tell them that the wedding isn't happening."

I didn't have any relatives in the small gathering, but Zeke had family present. A few cousins, an aunt, an uncle, and most importantly, his mother.

I felt my heart galloping inside my chest as I tilted my head and looked up at him. "This can't be what you really want, Zeke," I said breathlessly.

He pinned me with an intense stare. "You're wrong. This is exactly what I've wanted for a long time now."

"I don't understand," I whispered, feeling confused, and half mesmerized by the look in his eyes.

"You will," he answered ominously. "Just marry me."

The last thing I wanted was to embarrass him, so I squeezed his hand. "Never say I didn't give you an out."

Zeke's certainty was like a balm for my nervousness.

I trusted him. I wasn't afraid of the consequences, but I was still concerned about the fallout for him.

"I don't need an out, Lia," he rasped into my ear. "I just want you to walk up this aisle with me so we can say our vows."

I nodded slowly. If that was what he really wanted, I'd be right beside him. "Okay. Let's do it."

It was hard to take my eyes off him as I moved into position to walk beside him. I'd never seen Zeke in a tuxedo, and he looked so damn handsome that he took my breath away.

"Relax," he insisted as we walked slowly toward the altar. "You're getting married, not walking toward a guillotine. I have a couple of packs of chocolate pudding and some blueberry in my pocket for you once this is all over."

I let out a startled laugh. Chocolate pudding was my jelly bean flavor when I was extremely sad, and blueberry was my sunny day, complete happiness choice.

"I wasn't really sure which one might be applicable today," he added.

I shot him a smile as we stepped up to the altar together.

Even though I knew this wasn't the conventional way a woman got married, I couldn't shake the feeling that something about this day suddenly felt...right.

It felt like Zeke was the man who was supposed to be by my side.

This felt like the chapel where I'd always wanted to get married.

It felt like all the people who really mattered were here.

It felt like I was wearing the wedding dress I'd always dreamed about.

The flowers were right.

Everything was...

I inhaled sharply as my eyes landed on the table next to the altar, right beside the minister who was about to have us recite our vows.

There, among the roses and daisies, were two photos that Zeke had obviously enlarged and framed.

The first one was a picture of my parents that had been taken not long before they'd died. It was my favorite because the two of them looked so happy.

The second was Grandma Esther in her favorite red Christmas dress, smiling at the camera. That one, Zeke had actually taken himself.

My heart squeezed almost painfully inside my chest.

I knew Zeke had done this because he'd wanted me to feel like I had family here, too, even if it was only in spirit.

He'd probably thought nothing of doing it because he was a thoughtful guy, but the gesture touched my heart in a place that I didn't even know existed.

Zeke Conner knew my soul like no one else ever had, and he'd never once used that knowledge for anything else except to make me happy.

"Blueberry," I said in a quiet voice. "Most definitely the blueberry."

We turned to face each other at the minister's request, and when our gazes locked, the hopeful, relieved look in Zeke's gorgeous eyes made my heart stutter.

"Are you sure?" he asked huskily.

I nodded. "I'm positive."

The whole ceremony went by in a blur, and before I knew it, Zeke was gently pushing the most beautiful diamond ring I'd ever seen onto my finger.

And then, for the very first time, Zeke Conner kissed me somewhere *other* than my forehead.

And it definitely wasn't the quick peck on the lips I'd been expecting.

My breath hitched as he wrapped a strong, firm arm around my waist, and then cupped the back of my head with his other hand.

My body was tight with anticipation by the time his gorgeous lips finally touched mine, and when they did, I felt like my whole damn world tilted just a little.

Zeke explored my mouth thoroughly, tenderly, and firmly. Like he was staking his claim and making me a promise at the same time.

By the time I wrapped my arms around his neck and kissed him back, I was fairly certain that nothing would ever be quite the same between Zeke Conner and me ever again.

Chapter 7

Lia

"This is amazing," I said with a moan as I swallowed the first bite of the wedding cake Zeke had chosen. "It tastes exactly like—"

"The salted caramel chocolate cake we had at a wedding a few years ago," Zeke finished. "Same bakery, same cake. You said if you ever got married, you wanted that damn cake. I made sure to find out exactly where it had come from and the name of it before we left."

I looked at *him* instead of digging into the triple layers of pure decadence on my plate. "You actually remember that? It was over three years ago."

I'd been Zeke's plus-one for his friend's wedding because he'd been flying solo at the time.

He smiled and stretched his arm over the back of my chair. "It's not like it was centuries ago, Lia, and yeah, I remembered. I even recall telling you that I didn't think there was a groom in the world who would argue with you about your choice. It was a damn good cake. Isn't that what you and Stuart ordered?"

I sighed as I finally turned my attention back to my cake. "No. He wanted white cake with lemon chiffon frosting."

I shoveled another bite into my mouth, and watched Zeke as he picked up his fork with a slightly troubled look on his face.

He took a deep breath. "Okay, that just seems so…"

I knew he was trying not to be rude, so I raised an eyebrow as I suggested, "Vanilla?"

He grinned. "Just remember that you said that—I didn't. But I could definitely argue that vanilla *can* be extremely…satisfying."

I squirmed a little in my chair. Was Zeke…actually flirting with me? I'd meant "vanilla" as in boring, but my groom's brain had obviously traveled in another direction. "You have a very dirty mind," I scolded.

He chuckled. "Hey, I'm a newlywed who's sitting beside the most gorgeous bride on the planet. Where do you expect my brain to be right now? I did warn you that I planned on trying to seduce you."

"You know I never took that seriously," I said in a loud whisper.

He leaned over and nuzzled my ear as he asked, "Have I ever lied to you, Lia?"

I nearly choked on my cake.

His lips caressed my ear softly, his warm breath teasing and gentle, but the simple touch almost made me fly out of my seat. "As far as I know, you've never told me anything except the truth," I answered, nearly panting my reply.

"Then why would I do it now?" he asked huskily. "Don't tell me that you weren't at least *slightly* hot and bothered when I kissed you. I think we both forgot that we had plenty of sets of eyes watching for a minute or two. Jesus, Lia! You get my dick so damn hard that I can't even think sometimes."

"Zeke!" I squeaked, and leaned away. "Your mother is right across the table."

The grin on his face was deliciously wicked as he straightened up and leaned back in his chair. "I think even my mother knows exactly what I'm thinking about right now, but in more of a PG version than X-rated." He picked up his fork again and scooped up the last of his cake. "The bastard should have given you whatever cake you wanted. It was supposed to be your wedding."

I let out a breath of relief that we weren't talking about his cock anymore.

His kiss had gotten me very hot and bothered. He'd smelled so damn good, felt so incredibly amazing, that I'd leaned into that embrace until I'd nearly drowned before we'd finally come up for air.

God, even his suggestion that I turned him on was almost more than I could handle. I'd almost melted into a pool under the table.

What in the hell is wrong with me? I've known Zeke Conner for half my life now.

"Thank you for remembering my favorite," I murmured.

"It was your wedding, Lia. *Everything* should be your favorite."

I blinked as I realized that up until this moment, there wasn't a single thing that *hadn't* been my favorite or my choice. "What about you?"

He shrugged. "I got the bride I wanted, which is a pretty big deal for me. Do you really think I give a damn about flower selections or the menu when you're here with me?" He didn't give me a chance to answer before he asked, "Did I tell you how beautiful you look today?"

"You did," I assured him. "About five times since the ceremony. Do you like the dress I chose?"

"It looks incredible on you," he replied in an earnest tone. "It looks like your style, and I happen to love your sense of style."

I snorted. "Sneakers and jeans?"

"Definitely," he replied immediately. "I don't think I've ever seen a woman who can fill out denim the way you do. That completely gets my—"

I slapped a hand over his mouth as I whispered loudly, "Don't you dare! If you have to talk dirty to me, do it later. When your whole family isn't a few feet away."

He raised his eyebrows as I took my hand away. "Promise?"

I rolled my eyes. "Yes. Although I'm not sure that this new, sexy, naughty Zeke Conner isn't a little more than I can handle."

"I have no doubt you can do more than handle me," he said huskily. "It's more of question as to whether or not you *want* to... handle me."

"Zeke," I said in a warning voice. For God's sake, I was ready to strip him naked and have sweaty sex on the table right now.

"Okay, I'll change the subject," he said agreeably. "Do you want to explain to me why you nearly did a runaway bride routine before the ceremony? You looked terrified, and I know you were ready to bolt. I didn't realize you found marrying me that damn daunting."

"It wasn't like that. I guess I just realized how one-sided this deal is for you. I'll get my inheritance at the price of your freedom."

"Do I look worried?" he asked lightly.

"No. And that kind of scares the hell out of me," I confessed. "You wouldn't even do a prenuptial agreement."

"*Kiss! Kiss! Kiss!*"

To my chagrin, the whole table was tapping their spoons against their champagne glasses and chanting for Zeke and me to lock lips.

Without a moment of hesitation, Zeke put a finger under my chin and tipped my head up as he grumbled, "I'm not getting *nothing*, Lia. I'm getting *you*."

I shivered as his lips met mine in a more intimate embrace than we'd shared at the altar. This one was a lazy, thorough exploration that made me breathless, and I couldn't stop myself from kissing him back.

He devoured, and I opened for him because I needed him closer, and my entire body responded like a fireworks show on the Fourth of July. Zeke filled every one of my senses, and I lost myself in his insistent, sensual assault.

Granted, it was a little strange to suddenly want to rip my best friend's clothes from his body so I could intimately explore every powerful muscle and every inch of his bare skin. But somehow, it also felt as natural as breathing.

A longing I'd never experienced gripped me, and it refused to let go.

"Zeke," I whispered as he finally released my mouth.

"Don't be afraid, Lia. Just let it happen," he said hoarsely.

"But we're friends. None of this is even supposed to be real," I answered shakily. I was having trouble separating reality from fantasy because of my reaction every damn time he touched me.

"Right now, we're married. I think we're a hell of a lot more than friends."

Let it happen?

Really, did I have any choice when Zeke kissed me like that?

"We should be able to make our escape pretty soon," he mentioned in a casual voice.

We'd decided that it was best if we lived at Zeke's place, and most of my clothing had already been sent there.

I nodded. "Back to your place."

"*Our* place," he corrected. "But we aren't going home. I packed some of your things, and they're in the car. We have to leave from here to get to the airport. There's a charter waiting."

I was dumbfounded. "Why are we going to the airport?"

He shot me a grin. "We just got married, Lia. We're going on our honeymoon."

I frowned. The last thing I wanted was a honeymoon. Stuart had arranged a trip to Dubai, which wasn't exactly in my top ten places I wanted to visit. Or the top one hundred, for that matter. So I was more than happy to just hang out at Zeke's place. "Where?"

"Playa del Carmen," he answered. "Maybe I should have asked you instead of making it a surprise, but I thought you'd like to go someplace tropical and relaxing after the stress you've been through."

I'd never been to Playa, but I knew it was close to Cancun on the Yucatan Peninsula, and since it was gloomy and rainy in Seattle, it sounded like heaven.

I sighed. "I'd love to go somewhere like that."

"We are going," he replied.

"But my shop—"

"Will be just fine," he interrupted. "You have a manager, and Ruby will check in every day. We can do as much or as little as you want in Playa del Carmen. Snorkel, boat rides, or swimming in the underground caves, the pool, the beach, zip-lining, exploring the Mayan ruins, and eating all the good Mexican food we can find."

I laughed. "You don't exactly have to twist my arm to spend time in the Caribbean." I was completely sold on the idea of a honeymoon now.

Luckily, I'd had to get a passport for my impending honeymoon with Stuart. It was also fortunate that Zeke's plans sounded a lot better than Stuart's.

I'd never had a real vacation, and I'd always dreamed of getting to Mexico.

"Good. Then we're off just as soon as we can flee," he said with a hint of mischief in his tone.

I noticed that the music had started, but nobody had gotten out of their seat yet.

"Nobody is dancing," I told him.

"They're waiting for us," he explained as he got to his feet. "Dance with me, Mrs. Conner?"

Zeke held out his hand.

My heart skittered as I looked up and saw him looking at me expectantly.

I wasn't entirely sure that our bodies being wrapped together was a good idea, but he was my husband now. At least for a little while.

I took his hand as I decided to take his advice and just let things happen.

Chapter 8

Lia

T he following day, I was basking in the sun on a gorgeous beach in Mexico, wondering how in the hell I'd scored such a fantastic honeymoon.

Zeke had put us in a resort suite with two bedrooms, and the luxurious accommodations had every available amenity.

Since we'd gotten in late last night, we'd both retreated to our rooms, and then slept until late this morning.

I wasn't sure if I was disappointed or relieved that Zeke hadn't continued his seduction attempts last night.

I turned my head to look at my new husband, who was in the lounger next to mine. My eyes fixed on the simple platinum band I'd put on his finger the day before. It winked brightly in the sun, and my belly clenched. *Hard.*

For some reason, I still couldn't quite grasp the fact that Zeke, the guy who had been my best friend for so long, was now my husband, even if it was only going to last for a little while. Now that the craziness was over, I couldn't seem to stop thinking about *that*…or *him*.

Zeke was in a pair of board shorts, his perfectly formed body on full display.

To put it simply, my new husband had the body of a god. My eyes roamed over every inch of his muscular chest, and I itched to touch the smooth skin that covered those ripped abs of his.

Tearing my eyes away, I reached for the fruity drink on the small table between us, trying to find some relief from the gnawing ache in my belly and between my thighs.

"It's beautiful here," I said after I'd guzzled a large portion of my cocktail.

The beach was private, and only used by the resort. So it wasn't really crowded. Zeke and I had our own little slice of heaven, even if there were other guests around.

"Are you thawed out yet?" he asked in a teasing voice.

"Almost." Seattle had been cool and rainy, so I pretty much felt like I was in paradise. "Thank you for this. I think I needed it."

"I think we both did," he agreed. "Honestly, it's been a long time since I've gotten away from Seattle."

Zeke worked so hard that I couldn't remember the last time he'd escaped, either. Sadly, I also couldn't recollect the last time he'd really laughed and had fun. We'd both been so caught up in our lives that I suddenly realized that in some respects, we'd completely lost touch of each other's personal emotions.

Yeah, we saw each other at the coffee shop because he stopped in fairly often in case I needed his help with the business. But when had we stopped going out together as friends, having fun together?

Thinking back, I guess it had all been different since Stuart and I had started dating.

"I've missed you," I said before I could censor my words.

"I missed you, too, Jellybean. A lot," he answered in a husky voice.

"How did we start drifting apart?"

"I'm pretty sure it began when you decided Stuart was the best thing that ever happened to you," he drawled.

"Did I change?" I asked curiously, knowing full well that I had.

"Yes. You seemed restrained, and you were never meant to be subdued, Jellybean." He shot me a rueful smile, but his expressive eyes were hidden by the dark sunglasses he was wearing.

I leaned my head back against the lounge pillow and closed my eyes. "I'm not even sure how or when it happened," I admitted. "Little by little, I just gave up disagreeing with him about everything, from my clothing to my hair style. It was just easier. And I started second-guessing everything I did."

"Why?" Zeke asked. "At one time, you'd tell the entire world to go screw themselves if they didn't like you."

I shrugged. "I think he knew how to manipulate my insecurities. I got to the point where I felt like being me wasn't good enough."

"He was so fucking wrong," Zeke growled. "You know that, right? Nobody should ever want you to change to earn their love and acceptance."

"I know," I replied. "But that's easier to see when the relationship is over than when it's happening. I guess I never really wanted to acknowledge that I was doing all the compromising."

In short, Stuart was an asshole. He'd criticized me every single day, and I let myself absorb every perceived fault he pointed out until I was a different version of myself. A Lia I really hadn't liked.

He'd been in control.

And I'd merely been…an observer.

I felt so damn lost that I wasn't sure I was ever going to find myself again. Not that I actually missed *Stuart*, but I'd let him call the shots for so long and dictate who I was as a person, until I'd lost…myself.

My eyes flew open as I felt Zeke put his hand over mine. "Everything will be okay, Lia. It's just going to take a little time. Your emotions were still raw when Stuart came along because you'd just lost Esther."

I nodded. "I think I've been feeling lost since the day she died. I was looking for something or someone to fill that void, and things with Stuart went well at first. He seemed empathetic about what I was going through, but things…changed."

"He sucked you in first with kindness, and then started to turn the tables?"

"Yes. He was incredibly charming in the beginning. He swept me off my feet, and made me feel like he really understood my grief, and I believed him. I guess I didn't see the red flags when they started flying. Or maybe I just didn't want to see them because he'd made me feel loved in the beginning. I think most insensitive guys probably suck women in first by pretending to be Prince Charming. I just hate myself for not noticing when things changed."

"Did he ever hit you?" Zeke asked apprehensively.

"He didn't physically harm me," I readily informed him. "Although it might have been easier to walk away sooner if he had. Since he just screwed with my head, I rationalized his behavior."

"Jesus, Lia. I'm so damn sorry you went through that."

For some reason, I desperately wanted to cry. "You tried to tell me that he was an asshole, but I wasn't listening."

"I didn't try hard enough," he said roughly.

"Zeke, it wasn't your responsibility. I had to wake up to what was going on myself before I could change it. It's way too nice here to talk about the past right now. Let's go cool off. You ready to go for a swim?"

He stood and pulled me up gently beside him. "It's going to feel like warm bath water compared to Seattle, even though it's not summer."

"You're definitely not going to hear me complaining," I said happily.

I glanced at the beautiful turquoise water before I lifted the coverup I was wearing over my head, and tossed it in the chair. I'd only owned one simple, black, one-piece swimming suit, so that was what I was wearing beneath it.

My body filled with anticipation as I bolted toward the water, kicking up some of the gorgeous, white sand as I called, "Race you!"

My actions were a little bit sneaky, but I deserved a small advantage. There was no way I was going to beat Zeke in a sprint without one.

He didn't catch up to me until I was in the water.

It was warm, but the shock of hitting the sea, and the feel of Zeke snagging my waist from behind, made me squeal.

"Cheater," he accused. "You always give yourself way too much of an advantage. I never had a chance."

I'd probably heard those words a thousand times before because I always cheated if I was racing Zeke. It was a very familiar situation, but somehow, it felt different, and lot more intimate this time.

I was in waist-deep water as I turned around and laughed. "All I did was run. You're just getting slow, Conner."

"You distracted me," he said as he grinned down at me, his chest and face already wet from the initial splash we'd made when we'd plowed into the water. "A guy can't possibly *not* be diverted when your beautiful ass is right in front of him."

He hauled me against him, and I trembled as he wrapped his powerful arms around my waist.

He felt so good. So warm. So damned…tempting.

Time stopped as his liquid-blue eyes pinned mine as though he was searching for something. My heart kicked against my chest wall.

"Zeke," I said breathlessly, not knowing what to say about the way he made me feel.

I hadn't felt this way since…

Since my twenty-first birthday. Exactly seven years ago today.

Same emotions, same longings, same desires, and exactly the same guy.

The only difference was…Zeke definitely wasn't backing away this time.

No. Not possible. I'd gotten over that silly crush a long time ago. It just feels similar, right?

Zeke was so close that I could feel his warm breath against my lips.

"You're so fucking beautiful, Lia," he rasped right before his mouth covered mine.

My body caught fire, and I wrapped my arms around his neck, savoring every connection of my fingers against his bare skin.

Carnal desire flooded my senses, and I couldn't get enough of his marauding mouth, so I pushed back, meeting every stroke of his tongue.

It felt so perfect, so natural that I wasn't even wary about letting him in.

The way that Zeke consumed me felt so right that I couldn't imagine it being wrong.

He was different, yet familiar at the same time. And I couldn't get enough.

I wanted to explore this new, sexy, sensual, covetous side of Zeke that drew me in like a magnet.

I clung to him like a second skin, and I didn't ever want to let go.

He touched me like I was the most necessary thing in the world to him, like he needed me just to survive.

It was urgent.

It was addictive.

It was totally seductive.

And completely all-consuming.

I was panting when he finally released my mouth, his lips trailing to the sensitive skin of my neck, leaving a trail of fire in his wake as he said huskily, "I want you so damn much, Lia."

Incredibly, I wanted him, too. More than I could express in words. "I don't understand this. We're supposed to be friends."

"Let it happen," he said roughly against my neck. "Don't second-guess the way we feel together."

I wasn't sure why I felt like I *had* to figure everything out when I knew Zeke was right. I *could* just let myself feel, because what I was experiencing was very, very real. Couldn't I just savor those unfamiliar longings without having to analyze the entire situation?

My core clenched painfully as Zeke's mouth brushed against my ear. My body was demanding satisfaction. And dammit, I wanted to climb up his muscular body until I got exactly what I needed.

I let my head fall to one side to give him access to explore. "This doesn't happen to me. Ever."

He grabbed my ass and pulled my lower body tightly against him. "This happens to me all the time. Every damn time I see you," he grunted.

I nearly melted as I felt his hard erection press against my belly.

"I never knew," I answered in a rush.

"Now you do," he answered abruptly. "The question is…are you game for a new adventure, a different dimension of our relationship?"

I knew he was asking me if I was okay with our friendship moving to a whole different level. "I'm scared," I confessed. "I'm not used to feeling this out of control."

"You'll have to get used to it, and trust me," he said as he slowly backed away, took my hand, and started to tug me into deeper water.

I leaped onto his back and pushed his head underwater playfully. "I've always trusted you," I told him as he surfaced.

I squealed as he lifted my body and tossed me so far that I was sputtering when my head was above the water again.

Zeke was there to lift me up and adjust my legs around his hips as he replied. "I want to make you come until you can't remember your own name anymore."

I ground my hips against his washboard abs as I melted, knowing that I wanted exactly the same thing.

For this stolen period of time, when we were alone in a place where we didn't know another soul, Zeke was the center of my world.

Let it happen. I heard his voice in my head, even though he hadn't spoken, and I closed my eyes and laid my head on his shoulder.

The way I felt was much too powerful to do anything else except enjoy the moment.

Chapter 9

Lia

Two days later, I found myself wondering how I'd never known that Zeke was actually a really romantic guy.

He didn't pile on overboard, sappy, fake, over-the-top charm like Stuart had in the beginning.

Zeke was romantic in an I-want-you-to-remember-this-day-or-this-experience kind of way that touched my heart because his thoughtfulness was genuine.

"I love it. Thank you," I murmured to him as I clutched at the pendant he'd just put around my neck, a delicate medallion that was carved in white gold, and inspired by the Mayan calendar to remind me of the ruins we'd explored all day. "You do realize I'm getting completely spoiled. You just gave me the most beautiful pair of earrings I've ever owned on my birthday."

I turned, threw my arms around him, and gave him a hug.

I was wearing those gorgeous earrings, and I hadn't taken them off since he'd gifted them to me right before he'd taken me out for an incredible birthday dinner. I wasn't sure I ever wanted to take them off. Number one, I loved them. They were diamond studs surrounded by a beautiful halo of diamond accents. Number two, they had to have costed a fortune, and I didn't want to lose them. They had a really good safety back, so I was more comfortable keeping what had to be several karats of diamonds in my ears, rather than risk getting them lost or stolen.

"It's about time to get rid of those trainer earrings, don't you think? And you could use some spoiling. It's just a few gifts, Lia," he said in an amused baritone next to my ear. He lifted me off my feet and twirled me around before he set my feet back on the ground.

I sighed happily as my feet found the floor. "Bite your tongue!" I scolded. "Those so-called trainer earrings have been my favorite for the last seven years, and I'm thinking about just getting a second piercing so I can wear them above these." I put my fingers to my earlobes, just like I'd done a hundred times over the last few days, just to reassure myself that the new earrings were still in place.

The trainer earrings he'd been referring to were a pair of small, delicate diamond studs that he'd bought me for my twenty-first birthday. Even those earrings had been a pretty pricey gift for a female friend on her twenty-first birthday, but I'd cherished them from the day Zeke had given them to me.

He smirked as I stepped back. "So what happens when I get you the next pair? Or the next five pair? I think you'll eventually run out of space to pierce."

I shook my head. "Don't. Two is more than enough. You've spent way too much money on this wedding, the honeymoon, my beautiful ring, and jewelry. No more gifts for at least five years."

"Yeah? I don't think so, Jellybean. We're going to have to negotiate on that one."

I smiled as I leaned against the counter in the efficiency kitchen of our suite, and watched him unlace his hiking boots. He'd unlaced mine, and pulled them off my feet before he'd given me my necklace. "We'll see. Right now, I'm pretty adamant about that five-year time frame," I answered.

"Okay," he quipped accommodatingly. "I'll hit you up for negotiations tomorrow."

I snorted. "Smartass!"

He turned his head and shot me a grin. "You know you love me anyway."

I knew he wasn't really expecting me to answer after making that statement. Zeke and I never talked about loving each other seriously. Okay, maybe when we were younger, we had said those words friend-to-friend, but not since…

My twenty-first birthday.

Come to think of it, he'd never given me anything as personal as those adorable earrings since then, either, even though every gift after that had been extremely thoughtful.

Zeke had always been generous when it came to birthdays, holidays, and other special occasions, but he'd gone from generous to completely insane over the last week.

He absolutely had to stop!

I fingered the necklace he'd just given me, and then wrapped my hand around the pendant.

To him, the necklace he'd just given me was just a keepsake or a memento from our outing today.

For me, it would always be a reminder of what it was like to be with a man who gave from his heart with no expectations, and just enjoyed being with…me.

"I'm starving," Zeke told me after he'd kicked off both his hiking boots. "I hope our room service gets here pretty soon."

"They said forty minutes." I'd placed our order as soon as we'd come in the door, since we were both famished. "It won't be long."

I watched him as he went to the fridge, pulled out a beer for himself, handed me a wine cooler, and then dropped a bag of something I couldn't identify onto the kitchen counter. "I'll leave these here in case you want some later," he told me as he closed the door of the refrigerator.

I leaned around his massive body. "Jelly Belly Cocktail Classics! That bag is huge. I love those, but I don't find them that often unless I get to a store that has a bigger selection. Where did you find them?"

He shrugged. "I ordered them and had them delivered. They must have gotten here today. I think you have some making up to do if you were deprived for a year or more."

I tilted my head and assessed Zeke's expression.

There was no humor in his voice.

No mischief in his eyes.

Making sure I had plenty of something I loved, but had given up for a long time, was obviously something he was deadly serious about.

Don't cry. Don't cry. Don't cry.

It would be silly to cry over jelly beans, right?

On the other hand, I wouldn't be bawling over the candy.

My eyeballs wanted to leak at the moment because Zeke had felt compelled to have them sent here just to make me happy.

God, how long had it been since a guy had given a damn about any of my wants or needs?

I didn't tease him or joke around because I didn't want him to think I'd ever take something so considerate for granted.

He was quiet as he walked into the living room area and sat down the sofa.

I seated myself on the other end of the couch as I said, "Because I don't get those flavors often, I don't really associate them with a particular kind of emotion or feeling," I informed him. "So I think from now on, any of those five cocktail classic flavors will remind me of you, and how happy I am right now."

His eyes searched my face. "Are you happy, Lia?"

"Yes. You have no idea how much." I took a swig of my wine cooler, set it on the coffee table, and moved closer to Zeke until I was snuggled up to his side. "Do you want to be my strawberry daiquiri and pina colada?" I teased.

He put his beer on the side table, wrapped his powerful arms around my waist and hauled me as close to him as I could get. "Hell, yes. I'll be whatever damn cocktail you want if you're happy and you'll stay exactly where you are right now."

I laid my head on his chest, savoring his warmth, his heady masculine scent, and the pure joy of just being this close to him. "You're the most amazing man I've ever known," I told him earnestly. "I have no idea why some lucky woman hasn't snagged you yet, Zeke. You're the real deal. The whole package. How have you managed to stay single when you're pretty much every woman's fantasy guy?"

He stroked a hand lazily over my hair as he said hoarsely, "I doubt very much if I'm every woman's fantasy, and maybe I'm still single because I was waiting for you, Lia."

I sighed, wishing that was the truth.

The last few days had been magical, everything a couple could want on a honeymoon. Well, minus the *sex part.*

Zeke was attentive and affectionate, but he hadn't pushed for anything more than I wanted to give.

Truth was, I *wanted* to give him everything, but I knew that was dangerous.

This new relationship is not even meant to be permanent, which scares the hell out of me.

Every moment I spent this close to Zeke was both heaven and hell. He made me happy, but I was terrified what would happen when it was over.

For me, every touch, every brush of our bodies, made me want to beg him to fuck me, but I'd been thinking a lot lately about his long-ago rejection on my twenty-first birthday. I wasn't sure why, but I could still see the look on his face when he'd told me he didn't want me.

Zeke wasn't a guy who played games, so when had that changed?

I didn't feel like things were make-believe anymore. We *both* wanted more, and I was convinced that Zeke would like to explore something more intimate. And I *really* wanted to know what it would be like to be with him.

I wanted the experience *without* the risk, but those two things went hand-in-hand when it came to Zeke.

"Thank you for today," I said softly.

"Was it the experience you hoped it would be?" he asked.

I smiled. "It was. I can't explain it, but I could almost feel the souls of the Maya there. Is that weird?"

He shook his head. "No. I felt the same way. Maybe because we'll never really definitively know what happened to them. A lot of people have their theories, but it's still a mystery. Maybe that's why those places are so compelling."

"I think you're right. So what's on the schedule for tomorrow?"

"Whatever you want. This is your time, Jellybean."

I lifted my head to look at him. "I want you to enjoy it, too. The ruins were something I wanted to explore."

"I have a confession to make," he answered in a sincere, mesmerizing baritone. "There isn't much I'm *not* going to like if we're together."

I melted from the heat in his eyes, and swallowed hard. *Sweet Jesus!* Was I ever going to get used to the way that Zeke looked at me like he wanted to devour me whole? "I'm willing to do just about anything."

"There's a catamaran trip I wanted to arrange so we could do some snorkeling."

"I'd love that," I replied excitedly. Honestly, I was good doing anything with Zeke, too, but the idea of getting into the water was pretty damn appealing.

He nodded. "I'll hook us up. And then we can go into town. I got another tip on where we might be able to get some more authentic Mexican food."

"Sold!" I said with a ridiculous chortle that I couldn't hold back. "You had me at 'snorkeling' but I think you knew that 'authentic Mexican food' was definitely going to seal the deal."

I watched as his expression changed, becoming more thoughtful as he looked at me intently. "Do you know how good it sounds to hear you really laugh, Lia?"

"Have I really been that bad?" I asked, knowing very well that I hadn't been the same person for the last year or two.

Had I completely lost the ability to find any joy?

I'd been miserable with Stuart, and the dynamics of that relationship *had* changed me.

Somehow, I'd forgotten how it felt to be with somebody who accepted me without criticism, without judging everything I did.

"You look happier," Zeke observed with a questioning look.

I *was* happier, simply because I was with him. "We were always like this when we were younger. I guess I just forgot what relaxation and fun was like."

"That won't happen again. I'll be here to remind you."

I sighed.

No more Stuart.

No more constant belittling or sarcasm.

No more demanding mother of my fiancé who never thought I was good enough for her son.

No more...fear.

No more...paralyzing insecurity.

I was finally starting to see how really bad things were in hindsight. I just wish I had wised up sooner.

"I nearly married him," I whispered in a horrified voice. "What was I thinking, Zeke? Was I so damn desperate for love that I was willing to turn myself inside out to make things work with him? Was I willing to give up myself to please him?"

Zeke tightened his hold on me. "He was a master manipulator, Lia. For fuck's sake, don't blame yourself. You'll get over him. You just need time."

Our eyes locked as I said, "I'm not in love with him anymore, Zeke. I'm not sure I ever was. I don't need to get over *him*. I need to get over the fact that he played me so damn well. I have to figure out what in the hell is wrong with *me*."

"There's nothing wrong with *you*," Zeke rasped. "It's his issue, not yours. He just caught you when you were vulnerable."

I wanted to believe what Zeke was telling me, but deep inside, I knew so much of what had happened with Stuart *was* my fault. "But I should have been strong enough to stand up for myself. I let him distance me from my friends, even you. We've barely seen each other for the last two years if it didn't involve the coffee shop."

I hadn't even known what was really happening in Zeke's life. I'd completely missed the fact that he had broken things off with Angelique, and my relationship with him had been almost...superficial during the time I was with Stuart. That hurt, considering all Zeke and I had been to each other over the years.

"I think I can take some of the blame for that, too," Zeke said, his gorgeous eyes reflecting more than a little remorse. "I didn't want to see you with Stuart, so I pretty much avoided us meeting outside Indulgent Brews. It was easier to just see you at the shop."

I frowned. "Why?"

"Because he had something I wanted," Zeke said in a husky voice.

I raised a brow, confused. Zeke was a man with qualities Stuart could never dream of having. "What did Stuart have that you don't?"

"He had *you*, Lia," he answered in a rough, raw tone.

My heart ached as I looked at the tense expression on his face. Zeke was as serious as I had ever seen him. "God, I just wish we would have talked to each other," I said in a rush.

He raked a frustrated hand through his thick hair. "Fuck! I should have told you that I envied what you were giving to a guy who didn't deserve you," he countered.

Was it possible that Zeke Conner had really been jealous of Stuart?

Immediately, I pushed that question from my mind, certain he'd only meant that he'd missed our time together. I understood, because I'd missed him, too. "None of this was in any way *your* fault, Zeke. I wanted to pretend that everything was great with Stuart. In the beginning of my relationship with him, I convinced myself that he was the one. But he never was. You know my insecurities better than anyone, and you've never tried to play on them. I guess it was unfathomable to me that somebody else would use them to manipulate me. I was an idiot."

"Nobody who really cares about you would *ever* play those head games with you, Lia."

"Stuart did," I answered, resigned to the fact that I'd *allowed* Stuart to do it. "He made me feel so small and imperfect, Zeke, and he turned things around subtly at first, so I didn't recognize what he was doing. But eventually, he'd messed with my head so much that I actually thought that I was lucky to have him. I believed that everything that went wrong *was* my fault. God, I even hated myself because I couldn't satisfy him sexually." I took a deep, ragged breath, my emotions so close to the surface that I couldn't seem to stop myself from letting them pour out of my mouth. "To be honest, even though I haven't had that many sexual relationships, I've never been enough for *any* guy. Sex has never been a big thing to me, so maybe that part of it *was* my fault."

Zeke lifted a brow. "Are you serious? Please tell me you don't actually believe that bullshit."

I nodded firmly. Maybe our sex lives was the one subject Zeke and I never talked about, but I'd come too damn far to stop now. "Something is wrong with me, Zeke. I've never really enjoyed anything intimate. Or maybe it's my stupid curvy ass—"

"Goddammit, Lia!" Zeke interrupted in a graveled voice. "There isn't a damn thing about your body that isn't completely desirable. In fact, every single one of your gorgeous curves has been getting my dick harder than a rock for years now. Has the thought ever run through that beautiful head of yours that your previous partners just completely sucked?"

I shivered as Zeke's nostrils flared, and his eyes narrowed as he pinned me with an angry gaze.

"I've been with three guys, including Stuart," I confessed, easily spilling my guts to the man who had been at my side for almost every traumatic event in my life. "And no, I haven't considered that. One or two guys, maybe, but after three, I have to assume it's me."

Zeke was my best friend. Why had I never opened up to him before? Was it because I'd been too damn humiliated to admit to a guy friend as hot as he was that I was a sexual dud?

Or…had I never broached the topic because I hadn't wanted to hear about *his* sex life?

"I don't orgasm. God, I don't even really enjoy it at all," I admitted.

"Never?" he asked in a hoarse tone.

"Not once when I was with someone," I admitted. Hell, I was way too far into this confession to hold back now.

"But you can get yourself off alone?" A muscle in his firm jaw twitched, and his gaze never wavered from my face.

"Yes," I replied truthfully.

I watched as Zeke closed his eyes and let his head fall back until it hit the wall behind the sofa with a loud *thunk*.

I wasn't certain, but the sound he'd released *right before* his head smacked the hard surface sounded suspiciously like a deep, tormented groan.

He was completely silent after his skull had collided with the wall behind him, and his eyes stayed closed. I could see his chest rising and falling rapidly every time he took a breath.

"Zeke, are you okay?" I questioned, slightly alarmed that he'd hurt himself.

His eyes suddenly popped open, and he skewered me with a dark, blue-eyed stare I'd never seen before. His glare was so intense that it made my heart lunge inside my chest. "There isn't one fucking thing wrong with you, Lia. Never has been. Never will be," he rasped.

Zeke had always been protective. Granted, he'd never been quite this fierce about shielding me from being so self-critical. Then again, my confidence had never been this blown to hell, either.

My heart ached as I recognized the fact that Zeke had always been there, that if I'd only reached out to him as my best friend, he wouldn't have hesitated to drag me bodily away from a man who was messing with my head.

"Don't," Zeke answered in a warning voice. "Don't start beating yourself up because you didn't see it while it was happening."

God, sometimes Zeke knew me so well it was almost unnerving, because I *had* been about to criticize myself up for being an idiot. I crossed my arms as I looked at him. "Then how do you suppose I forgive myself for nearly marrying the biggest asshole in Washington state?" I questioned as I raised a brow.

A slow grin formed on his face before he suggested, "Remind yourself that you were smart enough to marry a better guy for you in the end?"

I let out a choked laugh of surprise as the tension in the room lifted. After I recovered, I teased him back as I drawled, "You, Zeke Conner, are way more than just a 'better' man. You're *every* woman's fantasy. There isn't a single woman on the planet you couldn't have if you wanted her."

I watched as his eyes narrowed before he answered gruffly, "Yeah, well, there's a problem with that theory because there's only one woman *I'm* fantasizing about, and *she's* not exactly eager to claim *me*, even if she is married to me."

My heart started to hammer so loudly that it was ringing in my ears as I answered, trying to keep my voice light as I said, "Maybe she desperately wants to, but she's afraid her new husband will be utterly disappointed."

"Then maybe she's delusional, but her husband is sincerely hoping the condition is just temporary," he grumbled.

There was a loud knock on the door before I could answer him.

I wasn't sure if I was relieved or disappointed as he got up and went to the door to get our dinner.

Chapter 10

Zeke

I *should have never fucking asked her if she could get herself off.* I panted like I'd just run a marathon, my hand still wrapped around my rapidly deflating cock after jerking myself off to fantasies of Lia's throaty moans of pleasure as she brought herself to climax.

"Christ! I'm so damn pathetic," I said to myself aloud as I leaned back against the shower tile, trying like hell to catch my breath as I let the warm water wash over my body.

I'd nearly lost it when Lia had admitted that she could, and obviously did, satisfy herself, even though no guy had ever done it for her. *Fuck!*

I hadn't touched Lia in a thoroughly sexual way since that first day we'd sprinted for the sea from the beach. God knew I wanted to, but the more I recognized how damn vulnerable Stuart had left her, the less I wanted to rush anything.

Okay. Yeah. My *body* wanted me to kick the whole seduction thing into high gear, but my brain and my heart were keeping my dick in check.

I wish I had paid more attention to *exactly* what Stuart was doing to Lia. The bastard had done a complete mind fuck on her until she wasn't sure if there was a single lovable thing about herself anymore.

It pissed me off that he'd been able to pick up on her insecurities well enough to be able to make her feel like she was...nothing.

Lia, she was *something*. Hell, she was *everything*. I knew I had to give her time to realize that all of the problems *had* been Stuart's. She was too damn smart not to eventually be able to internalize that truth in addition to just recognizing it.

"You need to be patient, Conner," I grumbled to myself as I washed up. "If she needs you to just be her goddamn friend, then do it. Lia is a hell of a lot more to you than just a fuck."

I slammed my hand against the shower control, turning it off much harder than necessary because I was irritated. Not with Lia, but with...myself.

I wasn't the type of guy who'd ever let my dick think for me, not even when I'd been a hormonal, horny teenager. So why in the hell was I having such a hard time—no pun intended—thinking rationally when it came to Lia?

"Because you want more than just her body," I rumbled, answering my own question as I stepped out of the shower. "Admit it, Conner—you want everything from Lia, and there's no fucking guarantee that she's able or willing to give it to you just because she agreed to marry you."

I grabbed a towel, drying my body absently, unable to stop torturing myself about all the shit that Stuart had manipulated Lia into believing.

If it wasn't so damn tragic, I would have laughed out loud about her assumption that she lacked passion. *Seriously? Lia?* There wasn't another person on Earth, male or female, who threw themselves into their life and the people she cared about with as much enthusiasm as she did. The woman did *nothing* half-heartedly. So I had no doubt that if she ever found a man who gave a damn about *her* pleasure, a guy she could trust, she'd be out of control in the bedroom, too.

Okay, so screw that whole part about her *finding* a guy who cared about her pleasure. She already had one, and I planned on being *that guy*.

Eventually.

As soon as I could convince Lia that I had no intention of being her *temporary* groom. I was done pretending that I was okay with letting her go if it meant she might find happiness with another guy who wasn't…me. In my mind, Lia had dated enough idiots who hadn't appreciated her.

Finally, after years of just being her best friend, it was *my* goddamn turn, and I wasn't about to blow the opportunity to make Lia mine.

If that made me a prick, I didn't give a damn, because nobody cared about Lia's happiness more than I did. "If she wants love so damn badly, then she'll have to take mine this time," I rasped irritably as I wrapped the towel around my waist. "Fuck knows I'm so damn crazy about her that my love wouldn't just satisfy her. Hell, if she actually decides she wants all of it, I'm half afraid it would suffocate her."

I'd tried to bury those emotions for so long, I wasn't exactly sure what the hell would happen if I just gave up trying to suppress the way I really felt about Lia.

Fuck! Lia wasn't ready for *that.* Not yet.

I strode through the bedroom restlessly, forcing myself to think inside the friend zone when it came to Lia, just like I always did. For now, that's what she *really* needed.

Lia had gone to bed early since we had a morning snorkeling excursion scheduled.

But I knew I was never going to sleep. I was way too wound up.

I went to the small kitchen of our suite, and pulled out a beer. I chugged it down, tossed the bottle and then grabbed a second one and screwed the top off.

"Zeke?" Lia's sleepy voice called my name softly, making me hesitate before I started on beer number two.

I turned toward that irresistible sound, and saw her standing at the entrance to the kitchen.

"You can't sleep? I couldn't sleep, either," she mumbled unhappily as she walked toward me.

My eyes followed her.

I recognized the red and white cotton sleep shorts and the matching tank top she was wearing. I'd packed them. Lia and I had been friends long enough for me to know what she preferred to wear when she was sleeping, even if we'd never shared a bed.

"You okay?" I asked.

She pulled out a wine cooler and tried to unscrew the top. When I saw her struggling, I snatched the bottle, removed it for her, and handed it back.

Lia looked adorably sleepy, her beautiful blonde hair tousled like she'd been tossing and turning in bed.

She hopped onto one of the kitchen counters, and then her eyes ran over my towel-clad body boldly, an action that made my dick hard almost instantaneously.

Dammit! I wanted her to want me, but the moment she did *anything* that even *remotely* indicated that she *might* be having dirty-minded thoughts about me, it was hell *not* to explore that possibility.

"I think I am okay," she answered, and then swallowed a portion of her wine cooler before she continued. "I messed up big this time, didn't I, Zeke? God, I nearly screwed up my entire life. I'm not exactly beating myself up, but I don't understand why I let it go for so long."

Her wistful tone and the sadness in her eyes nearly sent me over the edge. "Not your fault," I snapped out. "And you got the hell out of the situation *before* you married him." In a gentler tone, I added, "I know you're trying to find a more rational explanation, but you're eventually going to have to forgive yourself and just move on. You were vulnerable, and Stuart is a twisted asshole. I think a lot of it was just timing."

She nodded absently, but continued on thoughtfully, "I think I was searching for…something, and I wanted it so badly that I ignored all of the warning signs. I'm not a stupid woman, Zeke, and I'm definitely not naïve. Hell, I don't know, maybe it was timing. Maybe I was just vulnerable. Grandma Esther was all I had left. Maybe I thought Stuart gave me some kind of stability when I felt like I was just drifting and dead inside. Did I really think he was going to be the one person I loved who was never going to leave me?"

Watching the tormented, confused expression on her face as she struggled to figure out why she'd made that mistake completely tore me up.

I got it. I'd been there when she'd lost Esther. I'd held her, wishing I could absorb her pain while every single one of her tormented sobs had driven a stake through my heart. Knowing that, experiencing that loss with her, how in the hell had she ever convinced me soon after the funeral that she was okay?

Oh, yeah, that's right. She *hadn't*. I'd been the one who had backed away from her because she met Stuart, and I'd been pretty damn busy licking my wounds over the fact that Lia had started dating someone before I'd had the chance to tell her how I really felt.

However unknowingly it had happened, I'd just been one more person who cared about her who didn't…stay. Maybe not physically, but *emotionally* I'd checked out of our friendship once she'd met Stuart.

Now, I understood what she'd been craving, and why she'd been so willing to cling to Stuart. *Fuck!* He'd been the only one *available*, and she'd had no idea he was full of shit. Could I really blame her for buying his bullshit at a time in her life when she'd been so damn defenseless and exposed?

First, her parents had left her, and then, the only other person who had loved her like a parent had passed away, too. Yeah, her *rational* mind understood that none of them had abandoned her *willingly*, but let's face it, sometimes the mind and the heart definitely didn't always communicate.

I put my bottle down on the counter and situated myself between her legs. I took her bottle from her hand, and put it down on the counter beside mine before I placed my hands on her hips. I let my forehead drop to her shoulder, my heart, body, and soul filled with so much sorrow and regret that I was nearly choking on it. "I'm so fucking sorry I wasn't there for you, Lia. I don't know what I would have done without you after Dad died, and there was never a time you weren't there for me back then. You needed a hell of a lot more from me than what you got after Esther died, and instead of being there for you, I just...checked out."

She wrapped her arms around me and squeezed. "I wasn't there for you, either," she said with a sigh. "I'm guilty of letting us drift apart, too. In hindsight, I should have fought to keep you close because you were the one person I trusted, but it just seemed easier to avoid any kind of confrontation about Stuart. Now, here you are, temporarily stuck with me for a wife just because you're the only one who always cared, and I don't know what to do anymore." She finished in a rush, confusion and pain echoing in her voice.

Just love me! See me, Lia.

I couldn't make *that* suggestion out loud right now, but I sure as hell was itching to say it.

Fuck Stuart!

Fuck the past!

Fuck the regrets.

Fuck all of it, and everyone else.

This was about us, her and me, and everything we should have been to each other years ago. For me, there had never really been anyone else *but* her. I'd just been too damn afraid of losing her completely, so I'd used any excuse I could find *not* to tell her how I felt. I'd continued to make up bullshit excuses...until I couldn't anymore. Until the day she'd nearly married an asshole because of my silence.

I jerked my head up, meeting her gaze as I gripped her hips tighter. "Give *me* a chance, Lia. Give *us* a chance. After everything we've been through together, don't you think we owe that to each other? I don't expect you to get over everything that happened with Stuart overnight. I'm just asking you to try to see me as something more than a friend. I know this attraction goes both ways now."

I almost regretted my words as I watched Lia's beautiful green eyes turn liquid with tears. She gnawed at her bottom lip nervously, and then shook her head slightly as she repeated, "I still don't know what to do."

It killed me to see my Lia look so damned indecisive. It wasn't like her. The Lia I knew rarely hesitated about what she wanted, and it took me a few seconds to realize that even though Stuart was out of her life, some of her insecurities still lingered.

It wasn't like I didn't know that Lia's stubbornness and strength wouldn't eventually triumph, but it still made my gut ache that Stuart had been able to crush her spirit in the first place.

"What do *you* want to do?" I was distracted by the feel of her soft body leaning into mine, and I almost groaned when she hesitantly threaded her fingers into my hair.

"Right now, I just want to be with you," she said softly. "I don't quite understand exactly what's happening, but I want you, Zeke. I'm just…scared."

Every protective, possessive, out-of-control instinct I'd ever buried when it came to Lia tried like hell to break free, but I squashed them down. This moment was too damn important to me to screw it up now. "It's just me, Lia. We've known each other for a long time. Don't you know that you never have to be afraid of me?"

"I'm not afraid of *you*. I'm afraid of the way I feel right now, and the last thing I want is for you to be disappointed. What if we try to change our whole relationship and it doesn't work out? What if we lose our friendship over it? I hated it when we weren't really talking. I don't want to go through that again."

"You could never disappoint me, Lia. Ever." The words came out of my mouth in a low growl. I wasn't Stuart. "When has our relationship ever been conditional?"

She shook her head slowly. "It hasn't. I'm sorry. I shouldn't have said that," she answered as a tear dropped to her cheek.

I swiped at the droplet with my thumb, and then lifted her chin. "Look at me, Lia," I cajoled, knowing that if I didn't push for what I wanted right now, she'd back off. I knew that she would because I'd done it myself way too many times *not* to understand that instinct to withdraw instead of taking a risk.

I wrapped my arms tighter around her waist, and waited until she finally lifted her eyes, and squarely met my gaze. "We have to be sure, Zeke," she said cautiously. "I'm not sure we can ever go back again if we change everything."

"I'm not about to change my mind, sweetheart," I warned her. "I've wanted you for way too long."

My smile grew wider as Lia leaned back and boldly shoved her index finger into my chest. "Don't you dare give me that damn panty-melting grin and tell me that you don't have any reservations, Zeke Conner. I'm serious. One hasty decision could change every-thing between us for the rest of our lives."

I could feel her resolve weakening, even though her fierce expres-sion remained unchanged. "Christ, I hope so, Lia," I grumbled against her ear as I pulled her body tightly against mine. "If I can't get my cock inside this gorgeous body of yours pretty damn soon, I think I might completely lose my mind."

"I really did think you were just saying that you wanted me to help me get my inheritance," she sputtered.

I shrugged. "I *did* want to help you, but I also meant every single word I said when I asked you to marry me. Jesus, woman, don't you recognize a desperate guy when you see one?"

My dick twitched as she licked her upper lip. "I don't think I do. Maybe because I've never seen one look at me like you are right now."

"Then you haven't been paying attention," I said in a gruff voice. "I've been looking at you just like this for a long time, Lia. You've just never noticed. Say the word, and I'll have you in my bed faster than you can blink. And I guarantee I'll make you come until you beg for mercy."

Her breath hitched as she searched my face. "Those are pretty big words," she said breathlessly.

I stroked a hand up her spine slowly, and then gently caressed the sensitive skin at the nape of her neck, savoring every second of desire that flared in her emerald eyes before I replied. "It's not that you can't thoroughly enjoy sex, Lia. You just haven't...yet. Say the word, and I'll make it happen."

I wanted to kiss Lia more than I wanted to take my next breath, but since I was also anxiously waiting for her to speak, I settled for tasting the smooth skin of her neck.

"Zeke," she murmured softly as her head fell back, allowing me access to any part of her skin that I wanted to explore.

That trust, and that obvious signal that she wanted a lot more than she was getting, nearly made me come unglued. I'd wanted to touch Lia like this for so damn long that it was a constant gnawing in my gut that never stopped.

"Say. The. Damn. Word," I demanded, every muscle tight as I stilled and rested my lips against her ear.

She was silent for a moment before she finally whispered, "Word."

All of the tension drained out of my body as I said huskily, "You'll never be sorry you said that, Lia."

Before she could utter another word, I lifted her up, my hands firmly gripping her gorgeous ass. She had no choice but to wrap those shapely legs of hers around my body as I carried her to my bedroom before she changed her mind.

Chapter 11

Lia

Every single negative thought flew out of my brain as I pressed my body against Zeke's. They were replaced with heat, desire, and anticipation, which were much more pleasant things to focus on at the moment.

I'd laid in bed for over an hour before I'd finally gotten up and found the reason for my sleeplessness in the kitchen. Denying that I was attracted to him definitely wasn't working for me. In fact, the way my body reacted to Zeke just from a single touch was something I'd never experienced before, and I'd been so tempted to explore that attraction that the compulsion was pretty much irresistible.

Maybe he was right. Maybe I wasn't really a sexual dud. Maybe I just needed...him.

I'd initially gotten out of bed to try to find something that would put me to sleep.

Ha! When I'd seen the sexiest man alive dressed in nothing more than a towel, sleep had been the furthest thing from my mind.

Just let it happen.

I relaxed as he let my feet touch the floor in the bedroom, but I kept my arms around him like I was afraid he'd disappear into thin air.

"I feel like I've waited forever for this," he said, his voice hoarse and unsteady.

My heart was kicking against my chest wall as I looked up and met his unflinching stare. "Me, too," I confessed. If we were about to get naked, I saw no reason to not be completely honest.

I'd wanted this man for over seven years. After my twenty-first birthday, I'd managed to bury those emotions, ignore them completely, but that desire was emerging with a vengeance.

He stepped back and reached for my tank top, and then pulled it over my head.

This moment felt so natural with Zeke, and I needed him to touch me so desperately that nervousness was the furthest thing from my mind.

"You're so damn beautiful, Lia," he said in a deep voice that rolled down my spine, and then branched out to every single nerve in my body.

My breath hitched, and I reached for his towel. "I want to see you," I answered. "I really need to touch you, Zeke."

"Not yet," he said sharply, nudging my hand away as soon as the towel fell to the floor. "If you do that, I won't be able to focus on what's really important."

I tried to step back so I could see him, but he picked me up way too fast and carried me to the bed.

"What else could be more important?" I asked breathlessly as my back hit the sheets.

He supported himself with his powerful arms as he hovered over me. "I want to see you come, Lia. It's just about the only thing I can think about right now."

His words made me shudder, and I moaned as his mouth covered mine.

I no longer cared about the outcome. All I wanted was Zeke, and it was worth any risk just to be with him like this.

His kiss was ravenous, hungry in a way I'd never experienced before.

He demanded, and I happily gave, losing myself as I tangled my fingers in his gloriously coarse hair.

I got drunk on his masculine, musky scent, breathing him in as I tried to absorb his essence into every pore of my skin.

I was finally touching him, and I'd never felt anything so seductive.

"Zeke," I whimpered as he finally released my lips so I could speak.

"Don't think about anything, Lia. Just feel," he commanded, his mouth leaving trails of flame as it moved down my neck.

His torso finally dropped down over me, and I loved the feel of our heated skin pressed together.

When he pulled away, I nearly begged him to come back.

Until I felt his hands cupping my breasts, his thumbs circling the hard peaks of my nipples.

"Yes," I hissed. "Touch me. Please. I need it. I need you."

I can't say that he was gentle. Zeke's firm touch coaxed every sinful sensation he could get from me.

My back arched as he took a hard peak into his mouth, his teeth scraping against the sensitive flesh as his fingers continued to torment the other nipple.

When he nipped, I squeaked, and then let out a tremulous sigh as his tongue stroked over the tip he'd just bitten.

The pleasure/pain of the action fueled my need, and I felt moist heat that had been simmering start to pool between my thighs.

Pressure started to build in my lower abdomen, and I felt that tension start to knot tightly from the pleasure of Zeke's relentless, sexy assault.

"I need…more," I said, not caring if I sounded greedy.

"I'll give you everything you need, sweetheart," he growled as his mouth traveled into the valley between my breasts, and then down to my abdomen.

He pulled the thin shorts from my body in a frenzy before he knelt between my legs.

Every inch of my skin felt like it was on fire, and my muscles were tight as I waited for him to come over me and fuck me.

But what I'd expected didn't happen.

Instead, he spread my legs wide, and I shivered as the cool air wafted across my vulnerable pussy.

I moaned as I felt his fingers brush against the pink flesh. "You're so damn wet, Lia. So damn responsive. So hot. I can't wait to taste you."

I startled. I suddenly realized *why* he was settling between my legs instead of getting on with the business of fucking me. "You don't have to do that," I said nervously. "Nobody ever has."

No man had ever put their mouth on me, and I was trembling with anticipation.

Stuart had hated oral sex...unless I was sucking on him. He'd never been willing to do the same. The other two men I'd had sex with weren't my boyfriends for very long, so I'd been just fine not getting that close.

And oh, my God, this felt really intimate.

My body quivered as I watched the voracious look on Zeke's face.

"I don't just *want* to. I *have* to, Lia," he said insistently. "Let me. I guarantee you'll like it."

"Yes," I moaned, helpless as he stroked a thumb through my slick heat lazily.

All thoughts of any kind of protest flew out of my brain as his tongue stroked over the quivering pink flesh. He owned it in one long, satisfying swipe.

"Oh, shit, Zeke. Oh, my God!" The words left my mouth on a whimper, and my hands speared into his hair as I held onto him for dear life.

He groaned against my flesh, and the vibration almost made me jump out of my skin.

I flopped back against the pillow and closed my eyes, letting my body just enjoy every sensual sensation.

I'd never experienced this level of intimacy, this much pure carnal desire. And I savored it because it was so damn good.

"Yes," I moaned. "Please."

I felt the knot in my belly begin to loosen.

Zeke put his hands under my ass and lifted me so he could explore every single inch of my pussy with his very wicked mouth and tongue.

He was brash, bold, taking what he wanted while giving me the most exquisite pleasure my body had ever experienced.

It was both torture and bliss every time he brushed against the small bundle of nerves that needed more attention.

"Zeke," I pleaded as I yanked on his hair. "Please. More."

I yelped when his teeth bit down gently on my clit, gasping as I finally got what I needed, his teeth and tongue playing my body like a violin.

My climax rolled over me like a freight train. There was no slow build, no real warning. My orgasm pummeled me as Zeke continued to lap at the juices that spilled from me as I flew over the edge.

"Oh, my God. Yes! Zeke!" I screamed as I fisted his hair to keep my body from flying into outer space.

When it was over, I was left panting and helpless on the bed as Zeke climbed slowly up my body.

I felt every movement, the connection of our bodies as he moved over me.

"You taste sweeter than I could have ever imagined," he rasped as his face moved into my line of vision.

I searched his eyes, but I couldn't see one inkling that he hadn't thoroughly enjoyed the act, but there was still an audacious lust glinting in his beautiful eyes.

I wrapped my arms around his neck as he swooped down to kiss me.

I tasted Zeke.

I tasted myself.

I tasted sinful, wicked pleasure.

And dammit! It was the sweetest, most delicious thing I'd ever tasted before in my life.

"Fuck me," I insisted as he ended the embrace.

"So demanding," he said with a hint of humor, though his eyes were so intent that they pinned me to the pillow.

I wrapped my legs around his waist. "Are you complaining?" I said as I lifted my hips to grind against him, my body ravenous to feel him inside me.

He reached down and positioned himself as he groaned, "Hell, no. I just want you to feel as damn desperate as I do."

"Mission accomplished," I said with a strangled sound of need.

"Thank fuck!" he answered.

With one swift, powerful movement, he buried himself to his balls inside me.

I gasped as he stretched me. It didn't hurt, but I was hard-pressed to take his length and girth.

"You're so big," I said breathlessly.

"Are you okay?" His voice was suddenly concerned.

"If you stop, I'll never forgive you," I warned.

He gently pushed the hair from my face. "This has to be good for you, too, Lia. If it isn't, there's no reason to keep going for me."

Tears welled up in my eyes as I met his gaze. His blue eyes were tempestuous and molten. But I could see that he really meant what he said, and it touched a place so deep in my heart that it took me by surprise. "You mean that," I whispered.

"Of course I mean it. I need you with me, Lia. If you're not, what's the damn point?" he grumbled.

I reached up and stroked his tight jaw. "You're so amazing, Zeke."

He was trying to say that my pleasure was his, and I already knew his pleasure was mine. We were so damn connected that it made my heart ache.

"Right now I'm impatient," he answered gutturally. "Talk to me, baby. Communicate with me. I have to know that you want this as much as I do."

The stretching sensation was no longer uncomfortable, and the need for him to fuck me was almost unbearable.

"I need you," I said simply, grinding up against him again. "So much that it might be you who needs to keep up."

"You have me," he ground out as he pulled back until he was almost out, and then thrust his enormous cock back inside me again with a little less force.

"Then show me," I begged. "Because there's nothing I need more than for you to fuck me like you mean it."

"I mean it," he grunted, and then began to move in a rhythm that left me mindless.

I moaned, my hands trying to touch every bare inch of his skin as he claimed my body in a way I'd never thought possible.

I felt him.

I tasted him.

Zeke surrounded me, and our bodies merged together like a long lost puzzle piece had slipped into that final empty space.

Every forceful thrust was both a relief and a torment, but my body responded to him with sublime gratification.

I reveled in every stroke of his cock, every one of his ragged groans, my hips lifting to receive him every single time.

My legs tightened around him, and I ground against him every time he buried himself deep.

We were so close, yet not quite close enough.

"Harder," I cried. "Don't hold anything back. Please."

The feel of Zeke was addictive, and my body greedily wanted everything he had to give me.

He obliged me by moving harder. Faster. His movements were so quick and rapid that I couldn't keep up. So I just hung on for dear life.

"Come for me, Lia. Let go." His voice was urgently persuasive, but equally demanding.

I felt like seeing me climax was his only mission in life at the moment.

I love you. God, I love you so much.

I wanted to say the words aloud, but I couldn't get them out of my mouth. I was suddenly catapulted into a powerful orgasm, a climax that tore through my soul as it ripped through my body.

"Zeke!" I cried out, unable to get another word past my lips.

My core clenched hard, and spasmed powerfully around his cock.

"Fuck. Lia. Yeah, baby, keep coming around my cock. Just like that. It feels so damn good," he groaned.

Our eyes locked, and I watched him, fascinated, as my chaotic spasms milked him to his own release.

His mouth came down firmly on mine, and I was speechless by the time we ended the frantic embrace.

I was a panting, shaking mess when he rolled me on top of him and held me, our bodies still slick with sweat.

It wasn't like I didn't want to say something, but I was so stunned that I didn't know what to say.

Zeke had just proved to me that I wasn't incapable of having really hot sex.

He'd been absolutely correct.

I'd just always been with the wrong guys.

Apparently, the only man who could awaken that kind of passion in me was…Zeke.

"Okay?" he asked in a deep, throaty voice.

"Definitely okay," I answered as I buried my face into his warm neck.

He stroked a hand over my back in a slow, soothing motion that was almost decadent.

I moved to his side and cuddled against him, reveling in the feel of his hot, powerful body against mine.

For the first time in a long time, I felt safe.

I felt wanted and desired.

I felt needed, without a single condition.

As I drifted off to sleep because I just couldn't seem to keep my eyes open, I felt like I was finally exactly where I belonged.

Chapter 12

Zeke

"**D**o you remember my twenty-first birthday?" Lia asked softly.

"Every second of it," I assured her. "Do you want me to tell you what happened that night?"

I was honestly hoping she didn't want to know. It was an event that we'd both avoided talking about for a long time.

Her, because she didn't remember a thing that happened that night.

And me, because I remembered everything.

She snuggled up to my side in the double lounger on the patio of our suite, and let out a thoughtful sigh.

We'd made it a habit to end our evenings out here, just listening to the sounds of the ocean and relaxing in the balmy nights. Hell, I was never happier than when I had Lia's gorgeous body sprawled alongside me or on top of me.

She's been so damn happy for the last several days.

Granted, the two of us were frequently drowning in sexual bliss, but it wasn't just…that. She laughed more, she hesitated less, and she wasn't really confused about the whole Stuart situation anymore.

And, oh yeah, she looked at *me* like I was the only man she needed. She was audacious and flirty when her eyes swept over me with a covetous expression that got my dick hard every single time she did it.

Lia had absolutely no problem reaching out for what she wanted right now. We'd barely gotten through the door of our suite after dinner tonight before she'd grabbed exactly what she'd needed, which, thankfully, had been me. She'd ridden me into oblivion in one of the chairs because she said I was taking much too long to get her into the bedroom.

Seriously? If that's what I got for being slow, I'd move like a sloth all the damn time.

"No. I don't need you to tell me, Zeke. I remember."

The light was too dim for me to completely see her face, but I could tell by her tone that she was telling the truth. "Why didn't you say something? You always acted like you didn't remember."

"I was mortified the next morning," she explained. "I felt like an idiot because I'd literally thrown myself at you and you'd told me in no uncertain terms that I wasn't what you wanted. You were wrong about me feeling different when I was sober, though. I was attracted to you, and I did want to have sex with you. I was just too afraid to say anything. I'm not sure exactly when it started, but it was way before that night. Although I did realize the next day that I absolutely had to accept that we'd never be more than friends."

"Jesus, Lia, I didn't say that I didn't want—"

"Yes, you did," I interrupted. "You distinctly said 'I don't want this and neither do you' that night. You couldn't get away from me fast enough."

I was momentarily stunned into silence. Obviously, she *did* remember most of the details. I took a deep breath and let it out slowly before I finally muttered, "You never mentioned it again. I thought you forgot the whole incident. Do you have any idea how difficult it was for me to turn that offer down, even though I knew you were drunk? I had to either back away from temptation, or screw up a very important friendship. It wasn't that I didn't want *you*. I just didn't want you unless you knew exactly what you were doing."

"I didn't want to mess up our friendship, either, and since I thought you'd never want me as anything more, I completely buried those desires. I never acknowledged it again, not even to myself, but I'm starting to think it never quite died."

My mind flashed back to the words that Jett had said before Lia and I had gotten married.

"I think if you could manage to find that part of Lia that wants you to love her, and she knows you're there to love her back, it might change everything for both of you."

Hell, if there was even a small possibility that she wanted me to love her, those emotions were already there for her, waiting.

My voice was rough and raw as I told her, "Had you given me a single sign that you wanted the same damn thing once you were sober, I would have reacted much differently. I just had to know that it wasn't the alcohol talking."

She let out a deep breath. "I think my lack of inhibitions was the only thing that allowed me to actually say it out loud, but it wasn't something I wanted just because I was drunk. I guess the point is, you were really the *only* guy I've ever wanted like this. I lost my virginity at eighteen, while you were away at college. I don't think either one of us knew what we were doing, so I chalked that sexual relationship failure up to inexperience. I think the second guy was more of an experimental boyfriend after my twenty-first birthday because any possibility of being with you was gone. And then there was Stuart. I think we both realize that Stuart was an enormous, two-year mistake that never should have happened. What I'm trying to say is that you're the only guy who has ever made me crazy with lust. Maybe I blocked it for years, but it's not like this has *never* happened before with you."

My head flopped back against the headrest of the lounger, and I let out a groan. "Fuck! I wish you would have given me some kind of clue."

I felt her shrug. "I didn't know I was blocking it. Not consciously. Not until I actually realized that you really did want me a few days ago."

"A few days ago?" I growled. "Lia, I've known that I wanted to make our friendship a whole lot more since I moved back from the East Coast after law school. Honestly, it was probably way before that because I know if you'd repeated what you said on your twenty-first birthday, I would have been all over that, too. All I ever had was one drunken proposition that I couldn't act on, without a single sober sign that you wanted me."

"I didn't want to go there again," she confessed. "I was grateful that we were still friends after that. So, somehow I managed to push even the idea of ever being intimate with you completely out of my head. I don't think those feelings ever completely went away, but if you were completely off-limits, I *had* to let it go."

I tried like hell not to think about every single missed opportunity I'd let slip by in the past. If Lia had said a single word about those emotions after her twenty-first birthday, we probably would have been here in Playa celebrating our anniversary instead of our honeymoon.

"Just for the record," I informed her. "No other woman has ever made me as crazy as you do, either. I'm not going to try to tell you that I haven't had enjoyable sex in the past, because I have. But not like this, Lia. Never like it is with you."

"Maybe it's just because it's so new for both of us," Lia considered. "We'll get bored eventually, right? This was meant to be temporary, so maybe by the time—"

I found her mouth in the dim light, and kissed her until I hoped she'd forget what she'd been about to say. When I was done, my voice was ragged as I said, "I don't want either of us to look at this relationship like it's an arrangement or temporary, Lia. For me, it's not. It's very real. Has it ever occurred to you that maybe the two of us should have been together all along? We've always been connected. Neither one of us have ever been happy with anybody else.

I've always intended to put every effort into making this marriage last. You and I...we fit, Lia. We always have. In every way."

She moved until she was half on top of me, threaded a hand through my hair, and put her head on my chest with a long sigh.

Christ! I fucking loved it when she did that, like she could never get close enough.

I knew that feeling. I put my hand on her gorgeous ass and the other around her shoulders, wanting to wrap her around me until nothing could separate the two of us again.

"Sometimes, the way we fit is almost scary," she confessed in a hesitant voice. "You've been part of my life for so long that I think I'm terrified to think about how it would be if you weren't. But I'm not sure the friendship thing would be enough for me anymore."

"I couldn't do it," I said honestly. "Not after we've been like this, not after you've been this damn close to me."

After this woman had seeped into every part of my body, my heart, and my soul, there was no damn way I could back away again.

"I want to be with you more than I want to keep being terrified that it won't work, so I'll put everything I have into this marriage, too, Zeke," she vowed. "I'll do everything I can to make you as happy as I am right now."

My heart felt like it cracked wide open. Hell, she thought she was happy? She had no idea what it did to me to know she was going to stop thinking of me as a temporary groom. That there was nothing about our marriage that wasn't completely real to either one of us. I kissed the top of her head. "Already there, baby."

Maybe things could have been resolved between us years ago, but it was possible that all those years of waiting were exactly what made things just as damn sweet as they were right now.

Chapter 13

Lia

It wasn't until the very last day of our honeymoon that I realized, and could readily accept, that I'd *always* been in love with my best friend.

After Zeke's humbling rejection of me on my twenty-first birthday, I'd just never wanted those emotions to see the light of day ever again.

It had been way too raw, and much too painful.

Any guy I would have ended up with would have been the *wrong one*, even if he'd treated me better than Stuart had.

I let out a happy, contented sigh.

Zeke had proved to me, over and over again, that there was nothing wrong with me. In fact, he'd seemed to enjoy demonstrating it on every surface of our gorgeous suite.

Maybe I wasn't completely recovered from my dysfunctional relationship with Stuart, but I'd be returning to Seattle a lot more like myself than I had been when we'd left.

Every time Zeke touched me, I became bonded just a little deeper to him, and even though I was scared, I didn't regret letting it happen.

If I was only going to get one shot at being with the guy I really loved, I was going to take it.

"You look deep in thought, beautiful," Zeke said as he came out onto the balcony where I was having my morning coffee.

I shook my head. "I was just enjoying the view. It's so beautiful here."

We had a glorious suite that faced the ocean, and it was calming to wake up to the turquoise-colored Caribbean, and the lush, tropical green foliage every day.

My eyes ran lovingly over Zeke's hard body and handsome face, wondering if I'd ever get used to the fact that this beautiful man was mine. His hair was mussed up because he'd just climbed out of bed, but he'd never looked more gorgeous.

I watched as he poured himself a coffee, and sat down at the table with me.

"How do you manage to look incredibly hot when you just rolled out of bed?" I asked him with a smile.

He shrugged his strong shoulders as he replied, "Probably the same way you manage to look so beautiful right now."

He said the words so sincerely that they flustered me. I reached up and ran a hand through my messy hair. "I have bedhead. You don't," I argued.

"I'm too damn distracted to notice," he grumbled. "All I can think about is how you look when you come."

I laughed. For some reason, Zeke could always throw me off-balance with his blunt comments.

"Mind out of the gutter, Mr. Conner," I teased.

"I guess I'm still disappointed that I woke up without you in my bed," he answered.

"Don't you ever want a reprieve?" I joked.

"Hell, no," he said with a grin.

God, I loved his wicked smile. It made me want to take my clothes off and drag him back to bed.

But I knew we had plans for the day. We had a full day planned, consisting of swimming in the underground caves, and zip-lining.

"I'm going to miss all this when we fly out tomorrow," I said wistfully. "It's been so perfect."

Being in Playa had been like a fairy tale. It mostly had to do with the man I was here with, but the setting had been…magical.

Maybe I was afraid that everything would change once we were back in Seattle.

"Nothing is going to change," Zeke said, like he'd just read my mind. "But I'll miss it here, too. Things will be crazy once we get back, but now that I have a life, I'd like to bring on another attorney so I can do more pro bono work."

I looked at him in surprise. "I didn't know you were still doing that."

Before my grandmother had passed away, I knew that Zeke had taken on a case from a nonprofit organization that helped turn over wrongful convictions. Once he'd become positive the man was innocent of the murder he'd been convicted of years ago, Zeke hadn't stopped until he'd gotten an "innocent" verdict in a retrial.

He shrugged. "I take as many cases as I can now. Unfortunately, there are more innocent people in jail than I have the time to defend, but those are the kind of cases a good defense attorney lives for, really. It's easy to put everything into a case when you're convinced the accused is innocent."

"God, you're such a good man. Not that I didn't already know that, but what you're doing is special, Zeke." He was a guy who could give someone hope when they really hadn't gotten justice.

He winked at me. "It's not like I need the money another paid case would have provided. My firm makes enough money."

I rolled my eyes. And…of course he wasn't going to take any credit for doing something amazing.

He continued, "Maybe bringing on another attorney is a little bit selfish, too. Now that I have someone I want to be home with every night, I'd like to stop working twelve or fourteen-hour days."

"Couldn't you have stopped doing that a long time ago?"

He nodded. "Yeah, but I was single, and I really had no reason not to work all the time. I love what I do, but now that I have exactly what I've always wanted, I'd much rather be home at night with you."

My breath caught because I really wanted him to be there, too. "I'd still like to open a second store once I pay you back."

"You already know I support your company expansion whole-heartedly, and you don't need to pay me back, Lia. We're married. What's mine is yours."

"I want to," I argued. "Please." It was important to me to be able to hand him a check. He'd trusted me when he'd turned over that much money to help me achieve my dream. "I want to start this marriage knowing I'm pulling my share of the load."

"Is that really what you need to do?" he asked, sounding slightly disappointed.

"It is," I confirmed. "Even if it's only a symbolic gesture now that we're married, I want you to know that the last thing I'm after is your money."

"I already know that," he said huskily. "Come here."

His eyes were beckoning, and I couldn't ignore the temptation. I rose, moved to his chair, and he promptly jerked me down onto his lap.

I put my arms around his solid, massive shoulders to support myself, and his strong arms wrapped tightly around my waist.

"Thank you for this trip," I said softly. "It gave me a chance to get my head on straight."

"Damn! I thought you were thanking me for all those orgasms."

I laughed. "Do you ever think about anything except sex?"

"When you're around…no," he answered bluntly.

I savored the feel of his body against mine. Just being with him felt so…right.

Maybe this whole attraction should have been awkward because we'd been friends for so long. Instead, things actually flowed like a natural progression of our relationship.

I'd known Zeke for so long that there was very little I didn't know about him. And vice versa. Adding the sexual part of our relation-ship had just made it seem somewhat different, but it hadn't really changed our friendship.

I tilted my head down to look at him, and my heart skipped a beat as our gazes met and locked.

There was something incredibly intimate about the moment, and there was some kind of personal message in his stare that I couldn't quite understand.

"Are you okay?" I questioned in a shaky voice, unable to stop trying to figure out the silent communication.

His eyes seemed to suddenly shutter, and the moment was gone. "I'm good."

Dammit! I knew he'd wanted to say *something*, but hadn't for some reason.

"I guess I should go jump in the shower and get ready to go," I said, unable to keep the longing I felt out of my tone.

I didn't want Zeke to ever feel the need to be guarded with me. Eventually, I'd make damn sure he felt comfortable blurting out whatever was on his mind.

He let me go as I stood. "Need somebody to wash your back?" he asked hopefully.

"Pervert," I accused.

"Tease," he shot back in an indulgent tone.

I folded my arms in front of me. "All I said was that I was going to get ready."

"Which means you're planning on taking off those pajamas. Anytime you're getting naked, I definitely want to be there," he replied.

"You're hopeless," I said in an amused voice.

"I like to think I'm hopeful."

I snorted, unable to resist him when he was in a playful mood. The need to be close to him was so strong that I said, "If you join me, you know we won't get out of here early."

"I can be quick."

I rolled my eyes. The two of us could never seem to get enough of each other.

I raised a brow. "Now that's something I might have to see to believe."

I slid through the door of the patio.

Zeke rose and followed me so fast that he grasped my hand on his way, and ended up pulling me toward the luxurious master bathroom.

Turned out that I was right, but I certainly wasn't complaining when we left our suite extremely late that day.

Chapter 14

Lia

Zeke had been right about nothing changing much when we arrived back in Seattle.

Really, nothing was different except for the scenery.

We didn't spend as much time together because we were both back to work, but once we got home, the craziness between us just continued on. Zeke and I had been back home for over a week, and we craved each other like we were still in Playa.

"You're quiet," Ruby observed as she arranged some of her amazing pastries in the glass case. "Is everything okay?"

My shop was small enough that I closed down for an hour during midday for lunch and restocking. Normally, I'd restock Ruby's pastries myself, but she'd stopped in to bring some heavenly Korean food for lunch.

We'd wolfed it down before I started getting things ready for the next rush of coffee-lovers.

My manager was working out well, but she had the day off. So I was running the shop solo today. I had several part-time employees, mostly college students, who worked the evening shifts until we closed.

"Stuart is coming by to pick up his ring and his mother's dress. He apparently wants to give them to his new fiancée."

Ruby slammed the full case closed. "Asshole," she snapped. "An engagement ring is special. They aren't made to be recycled."

I shrugged. "He doesn't feel the same way. And I have no problem returning it. I never really liked it, and it certainly doesn't have any sentimental value." The ring was gaudy, ostentatious, and expensive, but it had never been my style.

My hand went reflexively to the ring currently on my finger, the gorgeous diamond that I'd basically picked out myself when Zeke and I had gone through catalogs. He'd said he just wanted to get an idea of what I really liked since a guy couldn't pick out a woman's wedding ring. Ha! He'd remembered every single thing I'd said about those rings, and put all my preferences together in one custom designed work of art.

Stuart, on the other hand, hadn't even requested a consult with me.

I kept replenishing cups and lids as Ruby said, "Are you going to be okay? It's the first time you've seen Stuart since the jerk left you at the altar."

I smiled at her. "I'm good. Stuart doesn't own me anymore."

"He never did," she answered adamantly.

"Maybe not," I agreed. "But looking back on it, I felt like a prisoner."

"God, I'm so glad you ended up with Zeke."

"Me too," I confided. "I just hope it lasts forever. I'm not sure I'd recover if it doesn't."

Ruby put a hand on her hip and stared me down. "Why wouldn't it? You love him, right?"

I nodded. "I do. But I wonder what will happen when we don't want to have sex every moment we're together."

"Lia, there's a lot more to your marriage than sex. You and Zeke have been friends forever. You know each other. You understand each other. If that isn't a great relationship, I have no idea what is. If you love him, it's perfect."

"I think I've always loved him. I was just in denial because I didn't think we'd ever be anything more than friends."

"I don't get it. Zeke adores you. And you're married to him now."

I startled as I heard someone pounding on the glass at the front of the store.

I turned my head to see Stuart waiting impatiently at the locked door. "He's here," I said, unable to completely brush off the twinge of fear that *zinged* through my body as I looked at him.

"We can talk later," Ruby said. "Are you okay being alone with him? Do you want me to stay?"

"This is something I think I need to do alone," I told her firmly.

Ruby nodded. "I'll be around. I'm nearby if you need me."

My heart swelled with love for the younger woman. Ruby had been a steadfast friend who never judged. She was just always… there for me.

I moved forward and hugged her tightly before I followed her to the door. "Thank you," I said in a quiet voice as I opened the lock.

She shook her head. "Don't thank me. You've done a lot for me, Lia. You gave me purpose when I needed it, and you've encouraged me to keep doing what I love. I'm happier, and I'm healing because of your friendship. You never have to thank me for being your friend."

Ruby had grown so much over the course of our friendship that she was almost unrecognizable as the timid woman who had offered to help me find better products for my store.

She'd blossomed tremendously because Jett had stood beside her, loved her unconditionally, and encouraged her every step of the way.

My eyes lifted to see Stuart right in front of me as I pulled the key from the lock.

My relationship with my ex had been a far cry from what I had now with Zeke, and what Ruby had with Jett.

I flinched as he pushed on the open door, nearly knocking me on my ass.

Ruby slipped out as Stuart barged in. I locked the door behind him since I had some time until I re-opened.

"I'll get your things," I told him stoically as I headed toward the counter.

"You're looking elegant as usual," he said in a sarcastic tone. "My God, Lia. When are you going to learn to present yourself as a woman instead of a sloppy teenager?"

I reached behind the counter and snatched up the bag with the ring and the dress.

It wasn't the first time I'd heard his criticism about the way I dressed for work. My place was a casual one and I was wearing a pair of jeans, a pretty jade sweater, and a pair of sneakers that didn't kill my feet by the end of a long day.

One of his biggest complaints had always been the ponytail that I sported to keep my hair out of my way while I was running around the store.

"Luckily, the way I look or act isn't really your concern anymore." I held out the bag, anxious to get rid of it...and Stuart.

He grabbed the ring box, popped open the lid to make sure the ring was there, and then shoved it back into the bag. "You can't blame me for looking for something better," he said in the snobby voice I hated. "Look at you. You have very little higher education, and you spend your entire day as nothing more than a...barista."

My temper started to flare, and that was something that I had never allowed to happen before when Stuart was berating me. I'd kept it buried to avoid an escalation of his humiliation.

I was afraid of him. I must have sensed that things could get physical if we actually argued.

The sudden realization of my true fears slammed into me with a force that rocked my body, and I tensed up more.

Stuart *was* an abuser. Maybe he'd never done anything except shove me around occasionally. But I was starting to understand how much the verbal abuse had scarred me, even though he'd never really hurt me physically.

For well over a year, Stuart had silenced my voice, made me fearful with subtle hints of retribution, and then made me doubt myself for thinking it might not be my fault.

When I'd been at the weakest point of my life, I'd let this asshole walk all over me, cheat on me, ridicule me, intimidate me, and then practically thanked him for doing it.

I'd forgiven myself for putting up with it, but I sure as hell didn't forgive *him*.

"I'd rather be a barista than a common bully," I shot back at him. "And there's not one damn thing wrong with hard work."

"I thought maybe you preferred to be a slut since you married another man within a few days of our wedding," he said angrily. "Not that you really have any skills at satisfying a man. That's one of the reasons I needed another woman."

It was so damn clear to me exactly what he was doing *now*, but it hadn't been quite so evident during our relationship because my head hadn't been in the right place.

In some ways, I'd wanted this final meeting for some kind of closure. Now I wished I'd just sent the damn dress and ring back to him and closed that door myself.

I felt the anger from every single mean word he'd ever said to me rise up to the surface, and before I could stop it, my hand flew through the air, landing with a satisfying *smack* as it connected with his face.

Fueled by fury, the slap had snapped his head to one side, and I felt nothing but gratification as I watched his face turn red with wrath.

"You think you found a better woman?" I asked angrily. "Well, I found a way better man, too. I'm glad I didn't marry you, and I feel sorry for the next bride you have lined up. I hope she has the balls to tell you where to shove every one of your opinions."

"You ungrateful bitch," he hissed. "You were nothing before I took pity on you."

"I wasn't nothing," I informed him as I strode to the door. "I was someone, a person I actually liked before I started to listen to you. And you tried to beat me down until I thought I was the one with the problems. But it didn't work. I wised up before I married you. If you hadn't called off the wedding, I would have."

Maybe Stuart had bent me, but he had never broken me. And his nasty comments about how lifeless I'd been in bed couldn't even touch me anymore. I knew better.

I shoved the key into the door. "Get out. We're done here," I said briskly.

"You fucking hit me!" His voice boomed around the small space.

"That was nothing compared to what you deserve. You have your ugly ring and your mother's dress. Don't ever contact me again." I lifted my chin and glared at him.

I'd be damned if I'd show him even a twinge of fear. I was done with that.

"You'll be lucky if I don't sue you," he snarled.

I shrugged. "Feel free. My husband is the best defense attorney in the country, so I'm not exactly concerned that I'd lose."

I opened the door and waited for him to exit. I wasn't about to flinch, even though my heart was racing with fear that he might try to physically hurt me.

Stuart was not a guy who let anything he perceived as an insult go unpunished, but he'd definitely made me pay enough for any of my perceived flaws he'd pointed out for over a year.

I'd never stood up for myself, so I wasn't sure if he'd back down, or punch me in the face. Since he'd proved to be a coward, it was highly possible he'd only harass women who he could intimidate.

My body was tense as I watched the indecision on his furious face.

I could tell he wanted to get his revenge, but because I wasn't willing to back down, he was hesitating. Obviously, he preferred his victims to be powerless and indecisive.

"Get. Out," I said firmly.

"Someday, you'll get what you deserve," he rasped as he left the store.

"I already did," I said softly as I quickly locked the door behind him, and released a sigh of relief.

I had Zeke, and maybe he was *more* than I deserved, but I never felt inferior when I was with him. He didn't hurt me. He smothered me with affection and compliments instead of criticism. He didn't try to make me into something I wasn't, maybe because in his eyes, there wasn't a single thing about me that had to change for him to care about me.

Tears of relief started to trickle down my cheeks, the product of a stark realization that I'd made a pretty lucky escape.

I leaned against the door and swiped away the tears. Now that I'd vented my suppressed anger, Stuart would never be allowed to take up even a tiny bit of space in my head ever again.

Chapter 15

Lia

I felt so much lighter the next day as I pulled into the parking garage of Zeke's penthouse, surprised to see that his Range Rover was already in his parking spot.

I'd knocked off early since my manager was on duty, and I picked up some groceries so I could make Zeke chicken parmesan with pasta, his favorite.

Cooking for him was never a chore since he went out of his way to let me know how much he appreciated it.

Other than the fact that I was afraid that our relationship would eventually end, I was happy.

After my encounter with Stuart, I was moving on. He no longer had any power over me, and I was done being afraid. Maybe I'd have some lingering self-doubt for a while, but I knew it would fade away.

I shut off the engine of my car, and gathered up the grocery bags.

I opened my door, but I hesitated to leave my vehicle as I spotted a familiar figure making her way to her car.

Angelique.

Here?

At Zeke's apartment building?

My heart squeezed inside my chest as I connected the significance of her presence with the fact that Zeke was here when he shouldn't be home yet.

Angelique and I had only met a few times in passing, but she was a woman who very few people would forget.

She was always immaculately groomed, and she reminded me of a woman who spent a lot of time on her appearance. Her long, dark hair was always perfect. She had the gorgeous bone structure of a model, with the height and slim body to match.

I let go of a shaky breath as she left, but I couldn't let go of the apprehension and jealousy that suddenly threatened to swallow me whole.

She was here.

Zeke was here when he should be at work.

She'd obviously been with him, right? Why else would she be here? I knew for a fact that she didn't live in this building.

My heart didn't want to accept the obvious explanation as I rode the elevator to the penthouse, but my brain couldn't ignore it.

My suspicions were validated as soon as I walked through the door.

"Lia," Zeke said hoarsely as he wandered out of the bedroom in only a pair of pajama pants riding low on his hips.

I put the groceries on the counter before he could reach for them.

Zeke didn't usually hang out in pajama pants unless he'd just gotten out of bed, and the thought of anybody else being in *our* bed with him except *me* made me absolutely livid.

"I saw Angelique," I said in a deceptively mild tone. "I thought we made an agreement to try to make this marriage work."

I started putting the groceries away, but I really wanted to just sink onto the floor and weep.

I knew what I was seeing, and I wasn't an idiot. Still, Zeke cheating on me just didn't feel…right.

I'm probably not the first woman to think that, or the last. No woman wants to believe her husband is sleeping with someone else.

"I don't know what you're saying," he said in a raspy voice.

I turned to face him. "I'm saying that I saw Angelique leaving the building. And you're home. In bed. In pajamas. Are you sleeping with her?"

"No." His answer was simple.

"Then why was she here?" A glimmer of hope sparked in my soul, but I was too defensive to let it turn into anything else.

I was surprised when he pushed me against the refrigerator, forcing it to close before he pinned me with his body.

"Are you seriously trying to say that you think I was screwing another woman?" he asked harshly.

I looked up at him. "I don't know what to think. She was here. And you're dressed...like that. You're never home this early."

He slammed a fist against the stainless-steel door of the fridge with a grunt of what sounded like frustration. "Jesus, Lia! After the last few weeks, you still don't believe that I fucking love you. There *is no* other goddamn woman for me. I know I wasn't the greatest friend to you while you were with Stuart, but I've tried to show you in every way possible how fucking sorry I am. I don't know how in the hell to convince you that I'm not going anywhere, that I'm crazy in love with you, and that there never has and never will be any woman for me but you. Christ! I'm incapable of cheating on you because the only woman I see, and the only female who gets my cock hard anymore, is you."

I lost track of how many curse words he'd managed to put into one declaration, but it didn't really matter. I was way too focused on the "crazy in love with you" part.

He'd been staring into my eyes as he'd told me that he loved me, and I felt the truth of that confession deep into my soul.

Zeke never lied to me. And I didn't think he was capable of it when he was looking into my eyes that way.

"I-I don't understand," I stammered. "She was here, and you're here with hardly any clothes on at a time that you're never home."

It wasn't that I didn't believe him, but nothing was making sense.

"You're pretty damn adorable when you're jealous, but it does piss me off that you, even for one second, considered that I might touch another woman," he commented softly. "I can't tell you for sure why she was here, but she used the gym and the pool here a lot while we were dating. I think she might have had a backup guy or two who she met here, but she sure as hell wasn't with me."

I felt my muscles relax. I was still pinned against the refrigerator by Zeke's warm body, but I wasn't trying to get away.

"I'm sorry. I'm so sorry," I blurted out. I felt terrible for even thinking that Zeke would betray me. If he'd wanted all this over with, he would have just told me. I'd gone with a knee-jerk reaction instead of trusting him.

"It's okay," he said as he moved back. "Maybe if I were in the same position, I might have initially assumed the same thing. It's not like I haven't made mistakes with you when I was jealous. Just know that I don't need to look anywhere else, Lia, nor do I have any desire to do that. No reason to when I've finally got the woman I've always wanted. I'd have to be a total moron to screw this up."

I finally got a good look at Zeke when he moved away, and I was dismayed when I saw that he was as pale as a ghost. "Are you okay?" I asked as I stepped up to him and put a hand to his face.

Oh, my God! He's burning up.

"Zeke, you have a fever," I said, worried as I looked him over steadily. I should have noticed earlier that his voice didn't sound completely normal.

He nodded. "I'm pretty sure I have the damn flu. It's been going around at the firm, but I don't usually get sick. It came on pretty fast. My secretary kicked me out of my own office because she didn't want to get sick. Not that I blame her. I feel like shit, and I didn't want any more of my employees sick, either."

His secretary adored Zeke like a son, so I wasn't buying that she kicked him out. No doubt she was worried and wanted him to take care of himself. "Oh, God, why didn't you tell me right away?" I asked, suddenly anxious because I'd made Zeke stand here and justify why he wasn't cheating on me when he was ill.

Now I understood exactly why he was home in a pair of pajamas, and in bed before I'd come in.

As long as we'd been friends, I'd never seen Zeke anything but healthy. He was right. He generally didn't catch anything going around.

I put my arm around him as I demanded, "Back to bed. You probably caught the flu because you haven't been getting enough sleep." We'd spent way too many late nights awake and drowning in sexual bliss since we'd gotten back from Mexico, and the crazy man worked really long days.

"Don't get too close, Jellybean," he ordered. "I'm contagious. I should have kept my distance in the kitchen. I can take care of myself for a few days. I don't want you to get sick."

I rolled my eyes. "Move," I insisted, staying beside him until he finally flopped back into bed. "I'm mad at you for not calling me the minute you found out you were sick. I could have gotten here before you did, even after a stop at the grocery store and the drug store. I'm your wife, Zeke Conner. I meant that whole 'in sickness and in health' part of my vows."

My heart squeezed as I looked down at him. He was even paler than he'd been in the kitchen, and the heat he was throwing off that massive body wasn't healthy. His voice was raw, and the poor guy looked like somebody had dragged him through hell and back. Unfortunately, since his symptoms had just started, it would get worse before it got better.

"I hadn't planned on even getting close to you," he admitted unhappily. "I want you to stay healthy."

My heart plummeted as I realized that Zeke's every thought seemed to revolve around me, even when he was ill, apparently. I sat down on the bed and stroked his wayward hair back from his forehead. "Get used to me being very close until you're feeling better. Did you really think I was going to let you take care of yourself? I work with the general public every single day, so don't worry about me. If I was going to catch it, I probably would have already."

He looked like hell, and it scared me. There was no way I wasn't going to be within hearing distance from him until he was better.

He scowled at me. "And if I don't want you close?"

Yeah, nice try, buddy, but you aren't scaring me off.

The dirty look didn't last long because he started to cough.

"Then I'll call your mom," I warned. "It's me or her. And if I do call her, it will pretty much be *both of us* since I don't plan on going away."

"Okay, now that's just cruel," he muttered when he finally stopped coughing. "Did you even hear me when I said that I was crazy in love with you?"

"I heard you," I answered. "And you have no idea how happy that makes me because I'm insanely in love with you, too, Zeke. But right now, I just want to get you better."

"Say it again," he demanded grumpily. "I've waited forever to hear you say you're in love with me. If I can't do anything about it right now, I *at least* want to hear you say it."

"I love you," I said obligingly.

He tried to crack a small smile. "I'm better."

I shook my head, but a small grin formed on my lips. "You're not getting out of bed. I was going to make chicken parmesan, but that's going to have to wait a few days. I'll make some soup, and see what I can find to take that fever down. If you're a good boy, I'll bring you a Popsicle," I teased.

He groaned. "It sucks to have the woman I love not see me as her stud."

"I don't need a stud," I argued. "Right now, I just want to see you healthy."

I started to rise so I could get him something for his fever, but he grabbed my hand. "Lia," he said, his voice sounding like his throat had been scraped with sandpaper. "I really do love you. I didn't mean to blurt it out like that, but you must have already known exactly how I feel."

His expression was so earnest that I felt like a vise was tightening around my heart. God, Zeke was beautiful, even when he was sick as a dog. I leaned forward and kissed him on his fiery forehead. "I didn't exactly know, but I think you made yourself perfectly clear. I really do love you, too. Now get some rest while I find some medicine, something to keep you hydrated, and make some soup."

I had a million questions I wanted to ask him, but I was more concerned about his health at the moment.

"If you get sick, I'm going to be really pissed off," he muttered as his eyes closed.

I smiled as I got to my feet, straightened up the bed, and shot him one last worried look as I went to find everything I needed.

He was asleep by the time I left the bedroom.

Chapter 16

Lia

Zeke was miserable through the first couple of days of his illness, and I soon discovered he was a *terrible* patient.

I had to put my foot down pretty hard to keep him in bed after the first day. By day two, he insisted he couldn't sleep anymore, and I'd had to practically sit on him to keep him in bed resting. I'd finally found a few movies we hadn't seen yet, and stayed with him to make sure he stayed put.

"I can't just lay here anymore, Lia. It's driving me crazy," he said on the afternoon of the third day. "At least let me go get a shower. I'm fine. Seriously. I'm not sick anymore. I just feel a little wiped out."

Zeke *was* better. His fever was finally normal when I'd checked it an hour or two ago, and he'd definitely gotten his appetite back. He'd wolfed down his chicken parmesan today like he hadn't eaten in months.

Really, I knew he was a very fit, healthy guy, and it wasn't surprising that he'd recovered fast. I'd probably been overreacting, but seeing him so vulnerable had scared the hell out of me.

I put my hands on my hips. There was probably no reason he couldn't get up. His fever was gone, and I knew he was getting restless and frustrated. "I'm going in with you," I insisted.

He grinned up at me. "Do you really think I'm going to object?"

"No funny stuff, stud," I said adamantly. "I just want to make sure you aren't going to fall down while you're in there."

"I feel fine, sweetheart," he answered as he threw the covers back. "I have since this morning."

I shooed him into the bathroom, and when he started to brush his teeth, I dashed back to strip the bed and put on clean sheets.

I hurried back into the bathroom and turned on the water of the rain shower, and then stripped off my clothes as I anticipated the warm water.

Exhaustion was taking over my body since I'd had very little sleep. Not that I couldn't have slept through the night, but taking care of Zeke must have triggered my memories of when I was taking care of Grandma Esther right before she died.

My dreams had gotten all tangled up, and for some reason, in a nightmare, I'd been taking care of Zeke when I knew he was dying, too.

It was really bizarre, but it had felt so real that I hadn't slept well since that first night he'd gotten ill.

Zeke was my entire world, and seeing him down and out must have shaken me up. A lot.

I stepped into the water that felt like a gentle rain, and sighed as I watched him finish shaving.

He was the hottest man I'd ever seen, even if he was recovering from an illness. Dressed only in another pair of pajama bottoms that clung to his hips like a lover, I'd never seen a more gorgeous sight than Zeke Conner.

I reached for the shampoo and body wash, making quick work of getting clean as Zeke entered the large space with me.

I'd dashed into the shower a couple of times, but it had been so quick that I hadn't really relaxed.

"You look tired," Zeke said unhappily as he got his entire body wet.

"I'm fine," I assured him. "It feels good to be able to relax. I know it's just the flu, but I was really worried about you."

Done cleaning myself up, I opened my eyes and reached for the soap that Zeke used.

"I know when I have it good. I'm not planning on dying anytime soon, sweetheart," he answered gruffly.

My heart sped up as I filled my hands with his soap.

Was that what I'd been afraid of all along? Was I manifesting the fear that Zeke would somehow be taken away from me, too?

That terror was irrational, and I knew it. He was young and healthy. But my parents hadn't been very old, and they'd been gone so suddenly that I'd never been able to even say goodbye.

My grandmother had been older, but she'd been in good health most of her life. Unfortunately, cancer was a greedy beast. It had swept my grandma away in a matter of months.

"I don't want to lose you," I told Zeke bluntly as I started to soap up his body. "I'm not sure I'd survive if I did."

"I know you've lost everybody you ever loved," he said in a patient baritone. "But you're not getting rid of me that easily, Lia. I can't stand to think about anything happening to you, either, but I'd rather be with you, and deal with whatever happens, than to be without you my entire life."

I looked up him steadily as I said, "Me, too."

Love was always a risk, but Zeke was worth taking a chance. I'd rather love him for as long as we both had with no regrets.

He closed his eyes and leaned back against the shower tile with a groan. "You're going to kill me off now if you don't stop."

I'd finished his back, and was running my hands freely over his muscular chest and gloriously toned abs.

One glance lower, and I knew why he was complaining.

His cock was rock hard, and doing a full salute.

I didn't hesitate to move my hand down to wrap it around the enormous, steely shaft. "I can take care of this," I told him in a sultry voice that I couldn't control. "Relax."

"Not happening if you're touching me, baby," he rasped loudly.

I stroked his massive cock, my anticipation building as I watched his face.

He looked hungry.

He looked frustrated.

And he looked like he was mine to pleasure.

Zeke had always been so eager to get inside me that I'd never gotten the chance to just touch him, taste him, and I relished the opportunity.

"I love you," I said as I dropped to my knees.

"Fuck! I love you, too, sweetheart," he said in a desperate tone.

His words rushed through my body like adrenaline, but there was also a gentle peace that was right there beside the excitement.

I rinsed the soap from his hard shaft before I took him into my mouth.

I started off lazily, my mouth and tongue savoring him before I finally started to apply some suction.

His body jerked as my movements got rougher and rougher, my hands grasping his tight ass to move at a steady pace.

A feral sound left his mouth as he tangled his hand in my hair and guided me. "Touch yourself, Lia. I'm not going to last long, and I want you with me."

I looked up and caught the carnal expression on his face. It spoke of lust, longing, and so much crazy love that my core spasmed violently.

His eyes were pleading, so I took a hand from his tight butt cheek, and slid it boldly between my thighs.

There was no hesitance from me. I wasn't shy about giving us both what we wanted.

My fingers slid through my wet heat, and I shuddered as I rubbed over my clit.

I was primed and ready, my body as tight as a bow as I found a rhythm that felt good, and stayed with it while I continued to swallow Zeke's cock.

I felt his hand tighten in my hair, and when I looked up again, he was watching me, his gorgeous blue eyes molten and burning with an incendiary heat that consumed me.

We connected without words, and Zeke didn't take his eyes away until his head fell back and an animalistic growl was wrenched from his mouth.

The sexy sound sent shockwaves through my body, and I sped up my fingers, stroking myself harder as I felt my impending climax.

I moaned around Zeke's cock, and the vibrations set him off.

"I'm done for, Lia," he groaned. "Move back."

Was he crazy? I worked too hard to coax him to orgasm. I wasn't going to give up the chance to taste it.

I swallowed hungrily as Zeke exploded, reveling in his essence as it flowed powerfully down my throat before I finally let go and found my own release.

"Zeke," I said with a moan as pleasure flooded my body and my soul.

I relished the hot water flowing over my body as I panted on the tile, one hand gently stroking Zeke's cock and the other still between my thighs.

He pulled me to my feet and wrapped his powerful arms around me as he said huskily, "Do you know how damn crazy you make me feel?"

"As crazy as you make me?" I asked, still breathless.

I still hadn't completely recovered, so I laid my head on his shoulder.

"Crazier," he rumbled as his hands stroked over my soaked body, as though he was afraid I'd suddenly disappear. "Let's get out of here."

I didn't protest as he turned off the water and we stepped out. He toweled us both off before we collapsed together on the bed.

He pulled the covers up, and I cuddled up to his side when he wrapped his arms around me.

"Are you okay?" I asked.

"Never been better," he teased. "Sleep, Lia. I'm not going anywhere."

I let out a sigh of contentment as my eyes drifted closed.

I slept a very long, dreamless sleep that left me feeling normal again by morning.

Chapter 17

Zeke

The next morning, I sat in my home office, feeling pretty much normal. Maybe I still didn't have the stamina I usually had—which isn't an easy thing for a guy to admit—but I knew I'd get it back after a day or two out of bed.

I'd been awake since dawn, and I'd finally left Lia fast asleep in our bed, hoping the dark circles under her eyes and the anxious look on her face would both disappear.

Shit! I really hated the fact that she was so damn afraid of losing somebody she loved, but then, I couldn't blame her, either. Pretty much every important person in her life was gone, and I'd probably be just as terrified as she was if all of my family was suddenly dead before I'd turned thirty.

The phone rang, and I snagged it from the charger.

"Conner," I said, assuming it was somebody from work.

"I'd like to speak to Lia Conner please," the male voice asked in a businesslike tone.

"This is her husband. She's not available." Okay, I was just a little bit edgy over the fact that any male was calling for my wife.

"Marvin Becker from Becker and Associates. I'm calling regarding Esther Harper's estate."

I relaxed. It was the estate attorney. "Zeke Conner. How can I help you? I guess you could say Lia is represented by my firm." Yeah, that was a total fabrication since I'd never be counsel for my own wife, but I really wanted to know why he was calling.

I heard a bark of laughter coming through the phone. "I know you by reputation, Mr. Conner," the gentleman said with humor in his tone. "But I'm pretty sure your wife doesn't need a defense attorney. My business is pretty benign. Can you just let her know that the estate is settled, and that I'm sending a check by courier? A package should arrive shortly with the monies owed, and I think she needs to read the codicil and a personal letter that I was instructed to give her after everything was finalized."

"Esther left a codicil?" I balked a little at the thought. "Why wasn't it given to Lia along with the will?"

"It's all in the package," he answered evasively. "The codicil wasn't effective until Ms. Conner's twenty-eighth birthday, and Esther requested that the codicil and the personal letter not be produced until that event happened. My job is to honor every request possible of a dying client. I knew Esther for years, so I also considered her a friend."

"Is this going to upset my wife?" I said with a protective growl. "Because the last thing she needs is more emotional turmoil. She's been through a lot in the last two years."

"I don't think it will," he said hesitantly. "In fact, it might help with clarity. That's about all I can say."

While I appreciated attorney-client privileged information, it still irritated the hell out of me that he wouldn't say anything more.

I hung up, and tried to figure out exactly what Esther had changed that would necessitate a codicil. Maybe Lia didn't give a shit about the money, but she'd loved Esther like a parent, and I knew that her grandmother making anything about their relationship "conditional" had hurt her. It wasn't about the funds or the things in the estate. It was the final conclusion by her grandmother that Lia wasn't okay exactly the way she was at the time of Esther's death.

"Good morning."

I looked toward the sleepy, female voice, grinning as I saw her smiling from the entrance to the office.

I was grateful that she looked much better and more rested than she had yesterday.

I stood up. "Coffee? I already made some."

She nodded and retreated toward the kitchen.

Because I was hopeless to do anything else, I followed her.

Unfortunately, she was no longer nude, and had pulled on a pair of pajamas very similar to the ones she'd worn in Playa—a pair of stretchy shorts and a tank top.

Hell, maybe that nighttime attire was made to be comfortable rather than sexy, but when Lia was wearing them, my cock didn't see anything other than the hottest lingerie in production.

"Sit," she demanded, pointing at the barstool at the kitchen counter. "I can get my own coffee."

I grinned, but I sat down. Hell, I was the last one who wanted to add to her worries, but I couldn't deny that her concern about my health was completely adorable.

She'd regained her previously feisty attitude, and having it all centered on concern for me wasn't exactly making me unhappy. I wasn't averse to letting her boss me around a little because I knew it was coming from a place of love.

However, I also wouldn't mind getting back to those looks from her that made me feel like she couldn't wait to get me naked. I looked forward to that.

"I'm feeling good, Lia. I'm going back to work on Monday." It was Friday, so that gave me a few more days to work from home and make sure that I was no longer going to infect anybody else at the firm.

She nodded. "I'm going back to the shop on Monday, too. But I plan on making sure you take it easy over the weekend."

I was hoping that meant both of us staying in bed naked, and trying to fulfill each other's sexual fantasies. I couldn't imagine a better way to get my stamina back.

I grinned as I watched her stand on her toes to grab a mug that I could have easily reached, and then fill it with coffee.

I knew her routine by heart, and I no longer cringed when she added a bunch of creamer to her coffee, and several spoonfuls of raw sugar.

"Do you want some Jelly Bellies with that," I joked after she'd added even more sugar than usual to her coffee.

She appeared to contemplate the possibility before she answered, "Maybe later."

She moved to the counter, her face so close to mine that I had a hard time not grabbing the back of her head and kissing her senseless as she said, "Do you know how incredibly sweet it is that you make sure you're always stocked up on my favorite candy?"

"That's not exactly a big deal," I answered. Hell, it was a lot more work for Lia to keep feeding me so damn well every single night.

"It's a big deal to me," she argued. "Sometimes the little things go unnoticed, but I want you to know that I do appreciate them."

"Like you staying home from your store to take care of me?" I questioned.

She'd arranged for her manager to cover for her without a second thought about upending her entire routine for me.

"You'd do it for me in a heartbeat," she pointed out.

Yeah, of course I would, but that wasn't the point.

I was saved from answering by the sound of the buzzer from the lobby.

It was the courier, and I told the receptionist to let them come up.

After signing for the delivery, I took the package into the kitchen.

"Who was it?" Lia asked curiously from a chair at the table. She was finishing her coffee, the mug nearly empty already.

I sat across from her. "Courier. It's from the estate attorney."

"Go ahead and open it," she requested. "You know more about all that legal mumbo jumbo than I do."

I pulled out the paperwork, handed her the check, and started to scan the documents as I told her, "Apparently, Esther left a codicil to the will. This is for you. It's personal." I gave her the sealed envelope that I already knew contained a personal letter from Esther.

I quickly read the simple codicil. Since it was only a few lines, it didn't take long. "Holy shit," I cursed.

"What?" Lia said anxiously. "Is something wrong?"

"No. Lia, she was always going to give you everything she had. She added this codicil that states as much. For some reason, she didn't want you to know until you had passed your twenty-eighth birthday."

She frowned. "Why? Why would she do that?"

I nodded toward the envelope. "Read the letter. It will probably explain."

I was tense as she opened the missive and pulled out a single sheet of paper. I watched her face as she read it aloud.

My Dearest Lia,

Please don't hate this old woman for wanting to see you happy after I'm gone. There was never any question that I wanted you to have everything I owned after I left this world. You've given me nothing but joy over the years, and you've been like the adoring daughter I never had. Even now, I can't imagine anyone giving me more comfort as I'm nearing the end of my life.

I'm so proud of the woman you've become, and all that you've accomplished, so I only have one concern.

It's become rather obvious to me that you and Zeke Conner belong together, but I'm afraid that will never happen. Neither one of you seems to want to rock the boat on your friendship. I'm hoping that if I give you a little push after I'm gone, you might start thinking about a more serious relationship with Zeke. If, by the time you read this letter, that relationship hasn't bloomed, I still hope you think about it in the near future.

I had my soul mate in your grandfather for many years, and I just don't want you to pass up your chance to spend your life with yours. Zeke is that man for you, Lia, and you're that woman for him. The two of you just need to stop being so stubborn and recognize each other.

Whatever you decide, just be happy, my sweet Lia. That's all this old woman ever wanted for you.

With All My Love Forever,

Grandma Esther

The kitchen was silent as Lia's voice suddenly stopped. A giant tear plopped on top of the letter she was holding. And then another.

Finally, she dropped the letter and looked at me. "How did she know?" she whispered tearfully. "I never said a word. God, even I didn't know until recently."

I moved to lift her up, and then sat back down with Lia's warmth cradled on my lap as I answered gently, "I'm afraid I was probably a little more obvious. Maybe you never noticed the way I looked at you, but Esther obviously did. And she knew your heart, Lia. She knew you weren't going to marry anyone unless you loved that person, money or no money, so I think she was just trying to push you closer to me."

Lia shook her head like she was still in a daze. "She never wanted to change me. She *didn't* think I wasn't good enough without a man. All she was trying to do was push me toward my heart's desire when I didn't see it for myself. She thought we were soul mates, Zeke. Yeah, maybe that's a little old-fashioned and over the top, but—"

"It's not, Lia," I interrupted. "I think she was absolutely right. I know I was too damn sick to do a very good job of explaining my feelings. I don't think the whole 'crazy in love with you' explanation was enough, so let me try it again."

My head was clear, and it was way past time that Lia understood that I wasn't just crazy about her, and I didn't just want her body.

I wanted it all.

Chapter 18

Lia

I didn't say a word as Zeke stood, carried me back to the bedroom, and then settled himself on the bed with my body sprawled half on top of him, and half beside him. It was a close, intimate position we slept in a lot, and I sighed as I laid my head on his still-bare chest.

It was obvious that he wasn't after some kind of immediate sexual gratification. Zeke had something on his mind, so I simply waited for him to talk, glad we were past situations like that last day of our honeymoon. I'd known he'd wanted to say something that day, but had still been guarded.

He took a deep breath. "I told you that I was looking for you when I found you in the hallway of the church on your wedding day. That I was determined to talk you out of marrying Stuart. But I never explained exactly what happened to me in that church that day, Lia."

"Tell me," I encouraged, wanting to know anything Zeke cared to share.

"I'm not sure I totally understand it myself, but it was like everything about the two of us suddenly became crystal clear to me.

The way we met, our friendship, all the things we'd been through together, and all of my feelings about you. Yeah, I'd desperately wanted to take our friendship to another level for years, but I suddenly realized that there was a reason why the two of us met in the first place, and that I'd blown every single opportunity I'd had to put us together the way we were supposed to be. I'm not big on the theory of fate or destiny. I think we can decide our own fate, but there are just some things in this life that can't be explained, and while I was sitting in that church that day, I realized you were one of those unexplainable occurrences. I knew we'd been meant to meet. I knew you *weren't* supposed to marry Stuart. I knew if I didn't stop that marriage, you wouldn't be happy, and I was positive that I'd never love a woman like I loved you for the rest of my goddamn life. And yeah, as crazy as it may seem, I believe we are soul mates, Lia. It was you, or it was nobody. I have to wonder if it was my dad or Esther trying to knock some sense into my head that day, before it was too damn late. Maybe that sounds a little nuts, too, but no stranger than having a major epiphany for *no* reason only minutes before you were due to walk down the aisle."

My heart tripped. "So you weren't joking when you said you would have bodily hauled me out of the church?"

He shook his head. "Hell, no. The sense of impending doom I felt that day wasn't going to stop until I knew you were out of danger. I couldn't let that ceremony happen, even if you hated me later for whatever I had to do. Call it intuition, call it whatever you want, but it was real, Lia. You said Stuart never hurt you, but my gut instinct was telling me that he was a threat to your safety as well as your happiness."

"I think he may have been both," I confessed. "He came by the shop to pick up his ring and his mother's dress. We had a brief confrontation, and I slapped him. I was so angry that I couldn't stop myself. I think the only thing that kept him from punching me in the face was the fact that I did stand up for myself. Had I stayed in that relationship as powerless as I had been, I don't think it's a stretch to say he would have eventually become physically abusive."

"Christ, Lia! Were you two alone? Why didn't you wait until I could be there with you?" Zeke rasped.

"Until that day, I don't think I truly admitted to myself that he was capable of physically hurting me. By the time he left, I'd vented my anger, and all I could think about was how damn lucky I was that I hadn't married him." I hesitated before I added, "I think I had the same epiphany you had at that church. The same sense of impending doom. Maybe we even had the same realization at about the same time that I just couldn't marry Stuart. Maybe I was feeling your panic, or you were feeling mine, even if we weren't physically together." Zeke and I were connected sometimes in ways I couldn't totally explain.

He stroked a gentle hand over my hair. "Don't ever meet with that bastard again unless I'm there. Jesus! I would have killed that asshole by now if I didn't know that I'd end up in jail and separated from you for the rest of my life."

I leaned up to look at his face. The intensity in his eyes skewered me. I brushed a soothing hand over his whiskered jaw. "He's not worth it. He's nothing to me anymore except a bully. Nothing he said or did before means anything to me. I have my shit together again, Zeke. I know who I am, and I'm exactly where I belong now."

He took my hand from his face, threaded our fingers together, and rested them on his chest. "You're my heart, Lia," he said huskily. "You always have been and always will be. I am crazy in love with you, but you're also part of me. Like—"

"Soul mates," I finished. "Before you interrupted me, I was going to say that I knew Esther was right. We fit, Zeke. We always have, and you're part of me, too. You aren't the only one who missed opportunities. I was searching for something that was right there all the time. I guess I was just too afraid to recognize it for what it was because I was too worried about rejection after what happened on my twenty-first birthday. But maybe all of that was meant to happen, too. It was a lot more difficult this way, but there will never be a day that I take what we have together for granted. I know just how damn good it is because I know what it's like to not have you."

"I need you to know that no matter how things might appear, or how obvious they may seem, there is never going to be a day when I so much as look at another woman with any desire to fuck her," he said gruffly.

I squeezed his hand. "I know. I'm sorry. That wasn't about you. It was about my lingering insecurities. I guess sometimes all of this seems too good to be true. It's hard to believe you're really mine, and that it's possible to be this damn happy."

I squeaked as he rolled until he was above me, my body trapped beneath his, and his beautiful blue eyes looking soulfully into mine as he said, "Get used to it, because my plan is to make you just as damn happy as possible for the rest of our lives. I want it all, Lia. I want to take you everywhere in the world that you want to visit on vacation. I want to be there for the good times, and hope that I can somehow make the bad ones a little better. And when and if you're ever ready, I want to be your partner when your body is swelling with our babies, and be right beside you when our kids come into the world. I promise I'll always try to be the best husband and father I can possibly be."

My heart skipped a beat or two as I thought about having Zeke's children. Our children. "I haven't even really thought about children yet, but I want us to have kids someday. You'd be an amazing dad."

He shot me a rueful smile. "No hurry. I'd rather have you all to myself for a while, and we have plenty of time for that in the future. But yeah, I've thought about having a daughter with your killer smile, and curly blonde hair. No doubt she'd wrap me around her little finger just like you do, but I could live with that. I'd definitely keep you two stocked with jelly beans so you could carry on that tradition."

"I'd love to have a little boy who looks just like you, too," I said with a sigh.

"Sweetheart, I'm perfectly happy where we are right now. Together. Anything that comes years from now would just be a nice bonus."

I opened my mouth to answer, but the words were stifled as his mouth covered mine.

Wrapping my arms around his neck, I got lost in Zeke's passionate embrace, any thoughts of the future flying out of my head.

I wanted to climb inside him, and never come back out again. He surrounded me in a love so complete that I couldn't get close enough.

"Zeke," I panted as he released my lips. "Fuck me. Now. Right now."

He pulled the sleep tank over my head, and seconds later, we were both naked.

"You know, this whole bossy thing you've got going on makes my dick so damn hard that I can't think," he rasped as we were finally skin-to-skin.

I wrapped my legs around his waist. "I'd be more than happy to give you a boner any time you want," I whispered against his neck. "I feel like I can never get you close enough to me."

"Do you know why it turns me on?" he questioned.

My body was taut with need, but I asked, "Why?"

"Because I know that nothing is ever going to break your beautiful free spirit. I know that you're feeling confident again. *And* I know that you fucking want…*me*."

He moved back and surged inside me with a force that made me suck in a breath as he lodged himself deep.

"Yes," I said breathlessly. "I do love you, Zeke. So much that it makes me crazy."

"I love you, too, baby, even if you do make me lose my damn mind."

I melted into him then, luxuriating in every frantic thrust of his cock.

Now wasn't the time for anything except the frenzy of joining us together. I could feel Zeke seeping into my body, heart, and soul. "More," I pleaded, my legs tightening around his waist.

He gave me more. Zeke gave me everything, and I felt myself hurtling toward climax as he grasped my ass, his cock pummeling into me with satisfying urgency.

"God, I feel like I've waited forever for you," I panted. "For us. For this."

Zeke was mine, and I felt it with every single movement he made, every fragmented breath coming from his lips, every rapid beat of his heart.

He claimed me as his with almost an animalistic ferocity that I reveled in.

And I took what I'd wanted for so damn long, my body finally imploding as I shuddered through my release.

"You were always meant to be mine, Lia," Zeke growled as he started to come. "Always. Fucking. Mine."

I clung to him, my breathing ragged as his words sank into my soul.

"And you're mine," I purred, my short nails digging into the skin of his back.

"Fuck!" Zeke exploded as he rolled me over on top of him, the two of us still connected. "You'll drive me completely mad by the time I'm forty, woman."

"Are you complaining?" I asked, still trying to catch my breath.

"Hell, no," he denied. "It's going to be a hell of a ride to insanity."

I smiled. It was incredible that loving Zeke could make me feel slightly vulnerable, yet so powerful at the same time.

He made me feel just as senseless as he did, but I certainly wasn't going to whine about those heady, exhilarating emotions, either.

My heart soaring, I whispered, "I should have known you were trouble from the moment you put Bobby Turner on the ground for trying to feel my boobs in ninth grade."

"I never knew his name, but I hated that little bastard," he said sternly. "You were only fourteen."

"And you were my hero," I shared with a smile.

"I always want to be your hero, Lia," he said earnestly.

"You never stopped being one to me," I answered honestly. "I love you, Zeke, with all of my heart and in so many ways it's almost terrifying."

"I love you the same way," he answered immediately. "But no fear, baby. We've always gotten through everything together, and we always will."

I hugged him tightly. "I know." I paused before I added, "What just happened wasn't exactly what I meant when I said I was going to make sure you took it easy this weekend."

I smiled as he started to laugh, a sound that boomed through the house so loudly that my heart started to gallop wildly.

It been a long time since I'd heard Zeke laugh like he was the happiest guy in the world.

Maybe I'd *never* heard that.

I squirmed until I was half sitting on top of him.

"I'm going to make you so happy, Zeke Conner," I promised. "We'll eventually forget all the hard stuff."

"I'm already happy," he rumbled. "And I'll have one more hard thing for you to deal with in another minute or so if you don't stop moving."

I put my head back on his chest. "You're resting," I chided.

"I'm working on my stamina," he argued.

I rolled my eyes. "And that's important right now...why?"

Honestly, I knew he was more than capable of going another round, but it certainly wasn't necessary.

He threaded a hand through my hair, and lowered his mouth to my ear. "Because there's nothing I love more than seeing my gorgeous wife looking at me like she can't wait to fuck me. I appreciate you staying with me in sickness, but your man is back in business, beautiful. There isn't a damn thing that's going to make him feel better than pleasing you."

Holy shit! I lifted my head, and got lost in the hungry, voracious look in his beautiful blue eyes.

How in the world was any woman supposed to turn down that kind of offer?

When it was coming from this man, I knew it was an unholy temptation I definitely couldn't refuse.

I'd make Zeke rest...later.

"Bring it on, stud," I dared teasingly.

He shot me the sinfully wicked grin I completely adored, and he did.

Epilogue

Lia

Almost Five Years Later...

I stood at the entrance to the living room, wondering how in the world I was going to break the news to Zeke.

Not that I thought for a single second that he *wouldn't* be happy, but this would rearrange a few of our life plans significantly.

Maybe I just hadn't completely absorbed the situation myself, so I wasn't sure what to think.

It wasn't like we wouldn't be able to go on the anniversary vacation to Playa del Carmen that was scheduled for next week, but that might be the end of our globetrotting days for a while.

Zeke and I had made sure we'd taken the time to travel, and hit all of the destinations we wanted to explore together over the last five years.

Our journey back to Playa for our fifth anniversary was purely sentimental, but we were both looking forward to revisiting our honeymoon destination.

I let out a soft sigh as I watched Zeke work on his laptop with a laser-focus that I'd come to know so well over the years. However, it was Saturday, and I knew he'd be done working the second he noticed my presence. The weekends were our time, and he'd never once let me forget that I always came first.

I'd been the one who had stepped out of the room an hour ago, so he'd obviously kept himself busy by working on one of his pro bono cases.

As promised, he'd hired new attorneys when necessary, and had devoted himself to working more and more with a nonprofit organization to help people who were wrongfully convicted. His firm had grown, and was flourishing, but Zeke did more management these days. He preferred to consult with his employees on all cases at his company, but personally defend the ones where he felt he could really make a difference, which made me love the impossible man even more, if that was even possible.

He still loved managing his own investment portfolio, and I knew he saw it as more of a challenge than a way to get even more ridiculously wealthy than he already was right now.

Zeke had more than tripled his financial assets since we'd been married. *Wait. Correction.* He'd more than tripled *our* financial assets. He got slightly pissy if I ever referred to any of those assets as his and not *ours.*

Of course, I'd had my own share of success over the years, too, so I could honestly say that I'd had some part in our financial success, albeit a smaller role than Zeke's.

Indulgent Brews now had a store in almost every major city in Washington, plus three different locations in Seattle. I was currently looking at expanding outside of the state. Maybe I wasn't as big as a few of the other giant coffee companies that had roots in Seattle, but I would be. I was just getting started.

Zeke liked to say I was a force to be reckoned with now, but he never seemed to mention that he'd been the cornerstone beneath that force, and that he'd supported me every step of the way. If I even mentioned that, he'd remind me that I was there for him whenever he made a major decision, so maybe he was right. We did have each other's backs, but I still thought I benefited a little more from that than he did since I picked his brain pretty often on business stuff.

However, no matter how much Zeke and I excelled with our businesses and our careers, neither one of us had ever lost track of what really mattered: our relationship, our life together, and our love, which grew even stronger every single day.

My breath caught as he suddenly raised his head, and those knockout blue eyes locked with mine.

"Hey beautiful," he said, his face lighting up the second he saw me. He closed his laptop and set it aside as he asked, "Everything okay?"

God, even after five years of marriage, the way he looked at me like I was the most important woman in the world still got my heart racing.

I shot him a tremulous smile as I sat down next to him on the couch. "I'm good."

Since I was on birth control and had been since long before we were even married, I'd thought I was just being overly cautious when I'd stepped out to take a pregnancy test. I hadn't wanted to tell Zeke because I knew there was very little chance that I was pregnant.

I'd just wanted to see the results to verify what I'd already thought was true:

I wasn't pregnant...I was just a few weeks late.

I wasn't pregnant...I was just a little moody lately.

I wasn't pregnant, and the morning nausea I'd been experiencing was just... stress.

I wasn't pregnant...I was just tired because I was working long hours.

Yeah. Well...

Turned out, I was wrong.

I *was* pregnant, and there was no rationalization in the world that was going to make that test come out any differently.

"I have to tell you something, Zeke, and I'm not sure exactly how to say it," I said hesitantly.

"Okay, this isn't like you, Lia. You know you can tell me anything. You're scaring me." He lifted a brow. "What? Are you okay, sweetheart?"

"I'm pregnant," I said in a rush before I could stop myself. "I know we didn't plan it this way, and we were going to wait a year until I got a store open in Portland. This screws up our whole schedule, and I'm not really sure how it even happened. I've never missed my pill. Okay, I'll admit that there was a day or two when I was a little stressed, and I didn't take it in the morning, but I took it that night. How can a stupid egg escape just from switching the time of day, for God's sake? Or maybe I'm just that tiny percentage of women who just got pregnant anyway, even though I'm on the Pill—"

"Don't," he said as he pulled me into his lap. "I was there when you got pregnant, too, and it wasn't your fault. I'm incredibly happy, sweetheart. I guess I'm just…stunned."

I wrapped my arms around him. "Me, too. I thought I was just late, and maybe a little queasy from stress. I've been really tired lately, so I just wanted to make certain I wasn't pregnant, but I am. God, I just didn't expect this to happen right now."

"How far along?" he asked. "Is it normal for you to be tired and nauseous? Is everything okay? Are you and the baby okay?"

"God, I love you," I said with a groan.

I should have known that Zeke's first concern would be for me, and our unborn baby's health.

Our schedule seemed to be the last thing on his mind at the moment.

He rocked me like I was a child, and the comforting motion felt so damn good. "Both of us are fine, I think," I informed him. "I'm probably around six weeks pregnant. I actually had to look it up on my calendar to figure it out."

"We need to find out who the best OB doctor is in this city, and get you in on Monday," he said, sounding firm, but slightly anxious. "We have to make sure everything is okay. Don't you need to be on special vitamins? What in the hell should you be eating when you're pregnant? Is there something I can make you that would help the damn nausea? And naps. I think you definitely need naps. Christ! Why didn't I look these things up before I needed the damn information? It's not like I didn't know you'd get pregnant someday."

I smiled. I certainly didn't need to be nervous or anxious. Zeke was feeling enough of that for both of us.

"I think we should hurry up and buy a house so we have a back-yard, and we need to get a room ready. Are we going to find out if it's a boy or a girl? Not that I really care, but it would be nice to know in advance, well, unless you want to be surprised. I'm okay with that idea, too. You'll be the one who has to carry this baby for months and then push it out, so it's only fair that you make that decision. I'll just...roll with it," he finished, releasing a large, audible breath.

I smiled even broader when I lifted my head and saw his harried expression. "I'm not delivering tomorrow, Zeke. We have around seven and a half months, and this baby isn't going to care if we live in a pent-house or a house. We won't really need that yard for several years. We'll figure everything out as we go along." I was starting to warm up to the whole idea of having Zeke's child now that I wasn't in shock anymore.

After all, it wasn't like I hadn't wanted to have a baby. It was just happening a little off-schedule, and schedules could easily be changed. Zeke and I were ready for this, even if my husband did appear to be in a momentary panic.

"Are you happy, Lia?" he questioned in an uncharacteristically vulnerable voice. "That's really all that matters."

I nodded. "Very. Maybe it isn't exactly the way we planned it, but it's still a miracle to me. It's *our* baby, Zeke. I could never *not* be happy about that. I guess we know that I won't have a problem conceiving, either. If it can happen while I'm on birth control, we can do it again without it."

Zeke and I had decided to have at least two children, if possible.

He stopped rocking and just held me. I put my head on his shoulder as he rumbled, "I'll take good care of you, sweetheart. Never feel like you're doing this alone. I love this baby already because it's ours. I won't say I'm not a little apprehensive about the pregnancy, but only because I know it's going to be unpleasant for you. I guess I'm not very good at seeing you uncomfortable or in pain, and knowing there's not a damn thing I can do about it."

"It will be fine," I assured him. "Pregnancy doesn't last forever."

"Maybe not," he grumbled. "But it may seem like it for you."

He put a gentle hand on my still-flat belly, and my heart nearly exploded with happiness.

I put my hand on top of his and sighed.

It was going to take some time for us to get used to the fact that we were going to be parents, but very little really scared me anymore.

I felt like Zeke and I had gone full circle together, and there wasn't much we couldn't handle in the future as long as we did it together.

"Are you hungry?" he asked in a worried voice. "You should eat. Maybe it will help the nausea."

I shifted on his lap and straddled him. "I'm not nauseous right now. It only happens in the morning, and I've discovered that crackers help. I'm not hungry for *food*, Zeke. The only thing I need right now is you."

My hormones seemed to be raging lately, and I couldn't seem to get enough sex.

He lifted a brow. "You sure? Maybe we should talk to the doctor first."

I nodded, amused by his uncertainty, an emotion that I rarely saw on his face. "It's perfectly safe, and all I really want to do is have sex. I think being pregnant just makes me feel excessively sexual."

"Then I'm definitely your man, sweetheart," he told me in a sexy baritone that made all of my hormones stand up and pay attention. "It's definitely no hardship for me to take care of that little problem as often as you want."

"You are and always will be my man," I said right before I leaned down and kissed him.

Zeke Conner was my one and only, and as he wrapped his arms around me, and held me protectively, I reminded myself how incredibly grateful I was that my first wedding had never taken place.

It was my *second* groom who was the keeper.

Honestly, it wasn't the wedding itself that really mattered at all.

Happiness was all about just marrying the right guy.

~*The End*~

Please visit me at:
http://www.authorjsscott.com
http://www.facebook.com/authorjsscott

You can write to me at
jsscott_author@hotmail.com

You can also tweet
@AuthorJSScott

Please sign up for my Newsletter for updates, new releases and exclusive excerpts.

Books by J. S. Scott:

Billionaire Obsession Series

The Billionaire's Obsession~Simon
Heart of the Billionaire
The Billionaire's Salvation
The Billionaire's Game
Billionaire Undone~Travis
Billionaire Unmasked~Jason
Billionaire Untamed~Tate
Billionaire Unbound~Chloe
Billionaire Undaunted~Zane
Billionaire Unknown~Blake
Billionaire Unveiled~Marcus
Billionaire Unloved~Jett
Billionaire Unwed~Zeke
Billionaire Unchallenged~Carter

Billionaire Unattainable~Mason
Billionaire Undercover~Hudson
Billionaire Unexpected~Jax

Sinclair Series

The Billionaire's Christmas
No Ordinary Billionaire
The Forbidden Billionaire
The Billionaire's Touch
The Billionaire's Voice
The Billionaire Takes All
The Billionaire's Secret
Only A Millionaire

Accidental Billionaires

Ensnared
Entangled
Enamored
Enchanted
Endeared

Walker Brothers Series

Release
Player
Damaged

The Sentinel Demons

The Sentinel Demons: The Complete Collection
A Dangerous Bargain
A Dangerous Hunger

A Dangerous Fury
A Dangerous Demon King

The Vampire Coalition Series

The Vampire Coalition: The Complete Collection
The Rough Mating of a Vampire (Prelude)
Ethan's Mate
Rory's Mate
Nathan's Mate
Liam's Mate
Daric's Mate

Changeling Encounters Series

Changeling Encounters: The Complete Collection
Mate Of The Werewolf
The Dangers Of Adopting A Werewolf
All I Want For Christmas Is A Werewolf

The Pleasures of His Punishment

The Pleasures of His Punishment: The Complete Collection
The Billionaire Next Door
The Millionaire and the Librarian
Riding with the Cop
Secret Desires of the Counselor
In Trouble with the Boss
Rough Ride with a Cowboy
Rough Day for the Teacher
A Forfeit for a Cowboy
Just what the Doctor Ordered
Wicked Romance of a Vampire

The Curve Collection: Big Girls and Bad Boys Series
The Curve Collection: The Complete Collection
The Curve Ball
The Beast Loves Curves
Curves by Design

Writing as Lane Parker
Dearest Stalker: Part 1
Dearest Stalker: A Complete Collection
A Christmas Dream
A Valentine's Dream
Lost: A Mountain Man Rescue Romance

A Dark Horse Novel w/ Cali MacKay
Bound
Hacked

Taken By A Trillionaire Series
Virgin for the Trillionaire by Ruth Cardello
Virgin for the Prince by J.S. Scott
Virgin to Conquer by Melody Anne
Prince Bryan: Taken By A Trillionaire

British Billionaires Series
Tell Me You're Mine
Tell Me I'm Yours

Other Titles
Well Played w/Ruth Cardello

Made in the USA
Coppell, TX
26 May 2021